End GAME

LISA SUZANNE

END GAME
VEGAS ACES BOOK FIVE
© 2021 Lisa Suzanne

Published in the United States of America by Books by LS, LLC.

ISBN: 9798713838140

This book is a work of fiction. Any similarities to real people, living or dead, is purely coincidental. All characters and events in this work are figments of the author's imagination.

Cover Designed by Najla Qamber Designs
Content Editing by It's Your Story Content Editing
Proofreading by Proofreading by Katie

End GAME

BOOKS BY LISA SUZANNE

A LITTLE LIKE DESTINY SERIES
A Little Like Destiny (Book One)
Only Ever You (Book Two)
Clean Break (Book Three)

MY FAVORITE BAND STANDALONES
Take My Heart
The Benefits of Bad Decisions
Waking Up Married
Driving Me Crazy
It's Only Temporary
The Replacement War

Visit Lisa on Amazon for more titles

DEDICATION

To my 3Ms. You're my End Game.

CHAPTER 1

"So what are you going to do?" Nicki asks.

We're at her house, obviously. I can't have an open conversation at my house since Michelle is still sucking the life out of it.

Our flight got in a few hours before the team's did. They take the bus as a team back to the practice facility, and then they all drive home their separate ways from there. Josh and Luke carpooled, so at least I don't have to worry about how Luke's going to drive home with a dislocated knee.

They should be back home in an hour or so, and I'm starting to get nervous. I don't know what state my husband will be in when he gets here, and I don't know exactly what my place should be.

"Just be there for him as best I can," I say. I keep wondering if I should tell Nicki about what I suspect is happening with my body. I don't have proof. It was less than eighteen hours ago that I first realized I'm late, and I'm too scared to work up the nerve to actually buy a pregnancy test.

I've never done it before. Though, to be fair, I've always double bagged it, so to speak. I've always been on the pill *and* made the guy wear a condom. With Luke, though, things were different. I thought I was fine since I was on the pill.

And now look where I'm at. This is why I double bag.

"I need Michelle out of my house," I say. I lean my head all the way back on the couch and stare up at the ceiling. "That's for damn sure."

"But the timing isn't great," she points out. "He needs to play nice with her now more than ever. He needs to stay on Calvin's good side because injuries are tough. Owners don't want to keep guys around if they aren't healthy."

I nod. "I get that. Luke isn't ready to be done. But between this injury and what's going on with Michelle, I just don't see how Cal's gonna say that they need to keep him."

She presses her lips together. "Yeah, it's not super likely. Would he play somewhere else?"

I shake my head. "He's been here his entire career. He's not interested in playing somewhere else."

"Even if it means he gets to keep playing?"

I lift a shoulder. "I don't know." More proof that I don't know him as well as a wife should know her husband.

A beat of quiet passes between us, and then Nicki says, "I have to tell you something."

My brows dip and I turn toward her. "What's up?"

She draws in a deep breath. "I wanted to tell you all weekend and Josh told me to wait and then Luke got hurt and I don't want to wait anymore."

A sense of alarm flitters through me. I don't know how much more I can handle.

"I'm pregnant," she blurts.

My eyes widen as the alarm turns into something else. My brain takes a half-second to put together that this is *good* news, not more bad news.

"Oh my God!" I shriek. "I'm going to be an auntie?"

Her eyes shine as she nods. "It's a honeymoon baby!"

I lean over to toss my arms around Nicki. Guilt presses on me as I hold onto my little secret suspicion.

"How have you been feeling?" I ask, more than a little curious as to what I might be in for.

She shrugs. "Pretty good for the most part. Tired and nauseous all the time."

"When are you due?"

"February twentieth."

I count backwards in my head. "So you're already three months along?"

She nods.

"When do you find out if it's a boy or a girl?" I ask.

"We're not. We want it to be a surprise."

"Are you hoping for one over the other?" I narrow my eyes and study her to see what she says.

She shakes her head. "As long as he or she is healthy, that's all I care about."

We're quiet a beat, and then I say, "I'm so happy for you guys. How many kids do you want?"

She laughs. "We'll start with one."

I need to take a test. Stat. I need to know if she and I are going through this together, if cousins will be born a few months apart. I need to know if Luke's going to father one child in December and another potentially in March or April. If I *am* knocked up, I have no idea when it might've happened. I don't remember missing any pills, but I know the pill isn't one hundred percent effective.

"What about you?" she asks. "How many kids are in your future?"

My eyes dart to the window almost involuntarily as I try to mask the fact that there might be one on the way. I'm not ready to just blurt that out before I even know if it's true. "God, I have no idea. One or two. Maybe three. Luke and I haven't really put a number on it."

"Aw, look at you! *Luke and I.* You want kids with him."

I lift a shoulder, glad I dodged the bullet of having to explain my current situation. "Well, yeah. I love him. I see him in my future. I don't see Michelle there, but we'll handle it if we find out it's his."

"How do you feel about it?" she asks.

"I can't fault him for anything he did before he and I met. And even after that. We didn't make any sort of real commitment to each other until after we got married."

Nicki giggles. "It's so weird to hear you say that."

I laugh, too. She's right.

"All right," I finally say. I stand. "I should head home. Debbie will be there cooking so at least I'll have a buffer between Michelle and me."

"You need me to come kick her ass?" she asks.

"I love you for asking, but no. You take care of that bun in the oven." I wink, bid her another congratulations, and then I head home.

I find Debbie stirring something at the stove. "That smells wonderful," I say.

"Beef merlot," she says, holding up a bottle of wine. "An old family recipe. You want a glass? I have some extra."

I pause. Oh shit. What if I *am* pregnant? I've been drinking lately. I never thought I might be. I feel fine—everything is totally normal.

I need to go get a test.

I make a face. "Thanks for the offer, but room temperature wine has never been my thing."

She laughs as she moves around the kitchen, and I glance at the clock. The boys will still be a little while, and there's a drugstore right up the road. "I need to run a quick errand. You'll be here a little while yet, right?"

She nods.

Can I even eat something that has wine in it? I have no idea. I know *nothing* about being pregnant or babies or children in general.

Although I *am* living with a pregnant lady, and there's another one across the street. If I need to know something, I'm sure one of the two could answer any questions I have.

Except one, I have no idea if I even *am* pregnant, and two, I'm not ready to tell anyone if I am. Least of all Michelle. Everything I know about pregnancy I've learned from her, and that hardly seems like the winning source of information.

I hop in the car and head toward the drugstore. I stand in the aisle with the tests for a few beats. I have no idea what I'm looking for. I even wonder if I should've worn some sort of disguise or at least a hat. What if someone sees me picking up a test?

I'm not thinking clearly. I'm tired.

All signs that point to what I think I already know.

I grab the test that looks the easiest to read with its digital screen letting me know if the results are positive or not. I take it up to the counter, and I'm lucky it's a teenaged girl behind it. She seems like she doesn't much care at all that I'm buying this when it's a huge freaking deal to me, and she barely even looks at me—surprising considering I'd be curious about every person who walked through my line, but that's me. I'm nosy by nature, I guess.

I pay for the test—the only thing on my ticket—and I take my bag and shove it into my purse. I think briefly about doing this right here in the bathroom of the store, but I'm not seventeen and stupid. I can do this in the privacy and comfort of my own home and still find a way to dispose of the evidence without anyone catching onto my secret.

I head home, and I rush upstairs to my bathroom. I read the instructions, but I don't have a lot of time. I scan for the basics, and then I do my thing on the stick. I cap it and stare at it as I wait for the results. A little hourglass flashes on the screen as the test works its magic, and my heart races as I stare at it.

It must be a million hours of waiting that in real time is only about three minutes.

And in those three minutes, a million thoughts run through my head.

I read somewhere once that an hourglass is a sign that life is fleeting—that pirates used them as symbols on their flags to scare their victims. I get that an hourglass symbolizes *time*, first and foremost, but it's that other symbolism that strikes me now. The sands of time will run out for all of us at some point, whether it's on our careers or a season or our entire life. It's inevitable. The one thing we really can't stop is time, yet it's such a limited, precious thing.

Whatever this test says when the hourglass stops flashing, one thing is certain. I want whatever fleeting moments I have left on this Earth to be spent beside Luke.

Yet I fear for us. This injury and whatever secrets are still held in his past are two things that have the power to come between us.

I'll do everything I possibly can not to let them.

Luke's words come back to me. *I want you to just hold out for the me you know. He'll be back, and we'll have our life back in a couple months, and we'll be stronger for it.*

He issued that warning before the injury. Does it still hold true? Will he be back? Or did the Luke I fell in love with change forever when Allen Hammond plowed into his knee?

That man he referred to when he said *the me you know* is my Prince Charming. That much I know.

The hourglass keeps flashing, and then a single word appears on the screen.

Pregnant.

CHAPTER 2

Tears roll down my cheeks. I'm not sure whether they're happy tears or something else just yet, but whatever the case is, this baby is Luke's without a doubt. I'm having a baby with the man I'm in love with.

Holy shit.

I feel a little dizzy at the thought of it.

I type *what do I do if I'm pregnant* into my search bar on my phone, and it says I should make an appointment with a doctor ASAP.

I don't even have a doctor out here.

Michelle's doctor was a little mean to me, but it was in the interest of her patient. Since it's the only doctor's office I even know about here in Vegas, I immediately call and book an appointment. They can't get in new patients until next week, and I suppose I'll wait to tell anybody anything until I've gone to that appointment and confirmed everything's okay. Then I'll have a due date. I'll have more information, and I'll be equipped to handle whatever Luke's response might be.

I draw in a deep breath, shove the test into the bottom of my purse, and hide my purse in my closet.

I stare at myself in the mirror.

I'm the same girl I was before I left for Denver, yet everything is different. Same dark blonde hair. Same blue eyes. But now I know something about myself I didn't before.

I hear the front door open and close. I swipe under my eyes, and then I hear my brother's voice. "Hi honey, we're home!"

I rush down the stairs. Josh is wheeling Luke in a wheelchair into the family room, where Michelle is already waiting on the couch with a sympathetic pucker on her face.

Josh helps Luke up from the wheelchair and onto the chaise lounge section of the couch, a place where I've laid with Pepper beside me a few times, by far the comfiest seat on the big sectional. I shove a few pillows under Luke's knee to keep it elevated and one behind his back before I sit beside him and study him.

He looks different. Still handsome. Still the man I fell in love with. But different.

His eyes are haunted and ringed with dark circles like he hasn't slept. He probably hasn't.

"How are you feeling?" I ask. I press a kiss to his lips—a kiss that isn't returned.

Just hold out for the me you know. He'll be back.

"Fine," he mutters.

"He's in a bit of a mood," Josh says, moving the wheelchair into a place behind the couch. His cheerful tone is a total contrast to Luke's rather sullen attitude.

"I don't blame him," I say. "Besides, I know how to cheer him up." I wiggle my eyebrows at Luke, but it doesn't even get him to crack a tiny smile. Michelle snorts across the couch.

"You can't just mount him with his knee like that," she says.

"Nobody asked for your opinion," I shoot back.

Luke sighs. "Can I just have some time alone?" he asks.

"Everybody out," Debbie says, her voice authoritative as her gaze falls to Michelle. She doesn't mean me...does she? "I've got my famous homemade chicken soup for you," she says. She sets a tray over his lap with soup and crackers along with a tall glass of chocolate milk. All of that sounds good to me. "Let's give Luke some space to eat in peace, and when he's ready, he will let you all know."

"Thanks, Deb," he mutters. He's doing a lot of muttering.

"I need to talk with Josh anyway," I mumble, and I follow my brother to the front door. "Is he okay?"

Josh shakes his head. "I've only known him for the last year, but I've never seen him like this. Football is his life, and it was just taken away from him for who knows how long."

"What can I do?" I ask, or rather, I *beg*.

"Give him a minute to sort out what he's feeling, and just be there for him. But don't take any shit from him. If you need me, I'm right across the street."

"Anything else I can do?"

"Do you have a guest room down here?"

I nod.

"Make it into your bedroom so he doesn't have to deal with the stairs," he suggests.

"Oh, good idea. Okay. Can I text you if I need any help?"

"Of course." He gives me a look of sympathy. "Luke will waver between wanting to be alone and needing you not to leave him alone. I know that won't be easy to judge when he needs what, but I can help. I know him pretty well. We don't want him to slip into a depression over this, but he very likely will. It's a big hit to him, especially given that it's the last year of his contract. Just be sympathetic and be strong, okay?"

I nod. "I'm nervous, Josh."

He hugs me. "I know. We'll be here for you, I promise. Let me pop home and say hi to my wife, and we'll be back in a bit. We can rearrange some furniture to make things more accessible down here for him."

"But we won't let Nicki move anything too heavy," I say, a touch of slyness in my tone.

He chuckles and rolls his eyes. "She told you, didn't she? I knew she couldn't keep it quiet."

I giggle before I toss my arms around his shoulders. "I'm so happy for you. Congratulations."

"Thanks, little sis." He squeezes me, and I don't know how I keep my giant mouth shut, but somehow I refrain from telling him that his baby will have a cousin only a couple months younger.

I've only been living with this news a couple minutes. I'm not quite sure I actually believe it just yet.

I give Luke some space to eat in peace while I go to work on the guest room. I can't do much since I'm guessing I shouldn't lift too many pounds, but I change the sheets on the bed and grab our pillows from our bed upstairs. I take our comforter, too, and I set shower supplies in the bathroom.

I tackle his office next, pushing the lighter things around to make it easier for him to move. I sit in his desk chair for a minute.

What does this injury mean for his sponsorships? What does it mean for next year? If he knows he'll just be cut after his contract runs out, will he even be motivated to work hard to get healthy?

These are all good questions. I make a note in my phone to email his agent tomorrow. He might have some of the answers I'm seeking, and since I'm his publicist, the agent seems like a great place to start.

I hear the doorbell along with Pepper's barking, and I find Josh and Nicki on the other side. Pepper calms when she sees familiar faces, and she scampers back to the family room to lie in front of the television.

Nicki has a bouquet of flowers with a *get well soon* balloon coming out the top. She brings her gift into the family room where we find Luke watching the game where he was injured. He's rewinding the play as we join him.

He watches as Hammond plows into him. Rewind. Watch. Rewind. Watch. Over and over and over.

It was a dirty shot. It was cheap. I've seen it too many times, and every time my reaction is the same: my stomach turns as I wince.

"The asshole didn't even draw a flag," Luke mutters.

Josh grabs the remote out of his hand and I clear away the tray holding an empty soup bowl beside him.

"What the fuck?" Luke protests.

"Don't do this to yourself, man," Josh says. He clicks off the television.

Luke blows out a frustrated breath.

"We brought flowers!" Nicki says brightly. Too brightly.

This is awkward as hell and I have no idea what to do.

"Thanks," Luke mutters.

"I'll take them!" I say as brightly as Nicki. I walk them over to the end table so we can all see them. "Can I get you anything?" I ask Luke.

He shakes his head, and Josh takes a seat nearby. "You hear from Dr. Charles yet?" Josh asks.

Luke shakes his head.

"Who's Dr. Charles?" I ask.

"Surgeon," Luke and Josh say at the same time.

"He's sort of our unofficial team orthopedic surgeon," Josh elaborates. "He has a private practice and specializes in sports medicine."

"He checked out my knee when we got back to the practice facility," Luke tells Nicki and me. "He has a surgery tonight but said he could get me in tomorrow or Wednesday. His secretary will call to schedule."

As if on cue, Luke's phone starts ringing. He holds it up. "And there she is." He answers the call, and we all listen to his side of the conversation, which mostly consists of grunts and *okay*s. When he ends the call, he says, "I need to report to the hospital tomorrow at noon and I can't eat anything between now and then."

Tears pinch behind my eyes. I want this for him—for him to start the healing process, to get healthy again—but I'm terrified of him going under the knife.

I can't believe how important he's become to me in the last couple months...and how important he'll be to our future now that I've confirmed my little secret.

"You've got this, man," Josh says.

Luke doesn't say anything, and my new goal for the night is to get him to unload some of what's inside and also to distract him from what's coming tomorrow afternoon.

CHAPTER 3

"How are you *really* doing?" I ask once we're alone...even though we're never *truly* alone with Michelle nearby.

"It hurts, Elle," he says softly, shortening my name by a syllable. He doesn't look at me.

"You need some ibuprofen or something?" I ask, not sure what to offer or what he's already taken.

He shakes his head. "I've taken some. They don't even touch the pain."

"What can I get you?"

He shakes his head and keeps his eyes on the blank television screen. "Nothing."

"I just want to help."

"I know you do," he says with a touch of frustration that reminds me how very much this isn't about me. "I just want to be alone."

"Even from me?" I ask with too much hope.

"I just want to be alone," he repeats.

So much for my goal of getting him to talk.

I grant him his wish, disappearing to my office for a while. But I can't work. I can't focus. Instead, I think good thoughts and send healing vibes to the man I love.

I give him an hour when I feel the need to check on him. And what I hear in the family room before I even step foot beyond the hallway stops me in my tracks.

It's laughter. Luke's. He hasn't laughed once—he's barely even cracked a smile in my presence—since he got hurt, and he's in there *laughing* right now. The sound of his laughter is a soothing balm to my soul, but then I hear another voice giggling with him.

I'm beyond confused.

I stride into the family room where I find Michelle sitting on the floor with her legs crossed. She's directly under Luke's feet, and she's adjusting his socks for him. That's *my* job.

"What are you doing?" I ask.

"Luke is so damn ticklish," she says, feigning total innocence. "His sock was twisted so I came over to help."

I didn't know Luke had ticklish feet. I didn't even look at his socks to notice whether they were twisted and I had no idea it would bother him if they were. I wonder what other things Michelle knows about him that I don't.

What things exist that *neither* of us are privy to?

"I can help," I protest.

Michelle stands. "All done." She claps her hands together and sort of wipes them like the job is done. "I'm going to bed. Luke, man up." She winks at him to let him know she's teasing him, and I hate how she's being so easy with him when I'm struggling to string a sentence together. "I'll see you in the morning."

I'm about to make some parting shot about when those test results are coming in, but I refrain. I don't want to piss Luke off, and especially not when he's actually smiling again.

I sit on the cushion where his legs are stretched out. "I fixed up the guest room down here so you don't need to try to tackle the stairs," I say. "You ready to go to bed?"

"I'd love a shower, actually," he says. He finally looks at me. "But I'm going to need some help with that."

"I'm here, Luke. For whatever you need."

"Yeah," he says thinly, his voice soft in case Michelle isn't completely out of earshot. "I guess it's in your contract."

His words stab my heart.

I know what he's doing. He's lashing out because he's angry about his injury, and I'm the closest target to take it.

I can't take it personally even though it hurts.

"That's right," I say. "It's the *in sickness and health* part of the marriage pact since I'm not aware of any other contracts you might be referring to." I smile sweetly, and he simply grunts in response.

Well if the reminder that our contract no longer exists since he ripped it up isn't enough, I guess I'll just have to work my magic in the shower.

And I try. Man, do I try.

I help him out of his clothes. He winces a lot. He mutters some curses. He grips onto the countertop for support—or maybe so he has something to clutch to help with the pain.

"Did they give you any painkillers?" I ask.

"They tried," he says.

"And you wouldn't take them?"

He just sighs in response. So it's going to be *that* kind of conversation.

I get it. He's a big, tough man. But that doesn't mean he can't take help when it's needed.

I help him slowly over to the shower, where the glass door is already open for him. It would be easier upstairs in our shower since it's big enough for two—or five—but that's not our current situation. I get undressed too, in part to try to take his mind off his injury and in part because I don't want to get my clothes wet from helping him.

"Do you want me to wash your hair?" I ask.

"I'm not a fucking child," he mutters, and I hand over the shampoo bottle. He's really in a mood.

He washes his face next, and most of his body. I kneel down to help him wash his legs and feet, and while I'm down there, I get a little idea in my head.

I glance up at him, and our eyes lock. A bit of heat passes between us.

Or, at least I *think* it's heat. I move toward his dick, ready to suck it to the back of my throat just to try to take his mind off things and give him a few minutes of happiness again, but he pushes me away.

He pushes me away.

I feel hurt. I feel rejected. I feel humiliated.

But this isn't about me, I remind myself.

So I finish washing him. I quietly get out of the shower and dry myself off, and once I have a towel wrapped around me, I help him dry his legs. He handles the rest himself because, in his words, he isn't a *fucking child*.

He brushes his teeth while I get dressed, and then I help him into his boxers and over to the bed.

He's silent through the entire process. I ask him little questions here and there, and I offer help where I think he needs it without assuming he can't do something for himself. And once he's in bed, I feel a tiny bit of sweet relief.

Once this surgery is over, I'll feel more of it.

"I'm going to sleep," he says, flicking off the bedside lamp.

"Okay." I set the television remote on his nightstand next to a bottle of water and his phone. "I'm going to work a while. I'll be back in a bit."

"'Night," he says.

"I love you," I say.

He doesn't say it back. I try not to feel hurt over that. Maybe he's already asleep or something, but somehow I doubt it.

I close the door behind me, and I set a hand on my lower belly as I lean on the wall in the hallway. And then I let the tears freefall down my cheeks.

CHAPTER 4

I can't decide which is preferable: feeling lonely because I'm actually by myself or feeling lonely because I'm sitting beside Luke. Either way, I bury myself in work for a while. I grab a snack, watch a show on Netflix, and then head to bed.

I slip into bed beside him. He's quiet, and I assume he's asleep. I turn away from him and face the windows of the guest room wishing things were different in this moment. We should be holding hands as we brace for tomorrow, and instead I feel like he keeps pushing me further and further away.

"I'm scared, Ellie," he whispers into the darkness. I'm nearly asleep, and for just a beat, I think I might've dreamed that he said those words.

"So am I," I admit, though my admission comes from a completely different place than his.

"I've been under this knife before. The recovery was brutal, and it'll be even worse this time with the dislocation and my age. I don't know if there's any coming back from this." His voice is soft, but I still hear the emotion in it.

Tears pinch behind my eyes. I'm grateful for this midnight confession in the dark. I'm grateful he's letting me in.

I turn onto my back then reach over under the covers to take his hand in mine. I lace my fingers through his, and I squeeze. "You're a fighter, Luke. If you want to come back, you'll find a way."

"Yeah," he murmurs. "But I don't know how much fight I have left in me."

"How come?"

"It's everything. You know? It's my age. It's Calvin making me feel like I'm not good enough, and it's Michelle and this baby trapping me into things I don't want with her. It's my family and the lack of support. It's feeling like an asshole for lashing out at the people I care the most about."

I hope he means me...but I'm not going to assume anything at this point.

"Let's start with your boss. How has he made you feel like you're not good enough?" I ask.

"I don't know," he says. "He just does."

"Any chance you're projecting your fears onto him?"

"Maybe," he mutters.

"Okay, what about the thing with Michelle?" I ask, moving onto the next part of his speech. "What if the baby isn't even yours? We should find out any day now."

"Right, but what if it *is*?"

"Then you'll be an amazing father. You care so much, and you're so kind and giving. You'll roughhouse and play and provide." I realize I'm telling him everything that's been flashing through my own mind since I took that test. I amend my thoughts to include the whole point of what we're talking about. "And you and Michelle will figure things out. You'll build a bridge for that baby. Maybe in different houses, though."

"I guess," he murmurs.

"When you mentioned lashing out at people..." I say, not sure how to ask if he meant *me*.

"I was talking about you. I didn't mean to push you away in the shower," he says, and I can't help but wonder whether he'd be confessing to these same truths if we were face-to-face in daylight rather than lying beside each other in darkness. "I just...I'm not in a place where I'm ready for that. Believe me, I want it. I want *you.* I love you. That hasn't changed, but like I once told you before, I become a different guy during the season. I *have* to. I'm focused on the game, and I can't afford distractions. But when I'm hurt, well, that becomes the center of my focus. I might be a different guy during the season, but I know I'm virtually unrecognizable when I'm hurt."

"You have every right to be," I say softly. "And I'm here for it. For you. I know this is the worst-case scenario, and I will hold your hand every step of the way."

Not just because I'm your wife. Also because I'm carrying your child.

I omit that last part. I can't tell him now—not because I don't want to, because I most certainly do. But because I need to get checked before I spring more news on him, especially when there isn't anything he can do as he goes into surgery tomorrow. It's just one more thing he doesn't need to worry about until I have a chance to see a doctor.

"And as for your family, your brother showed up at the ER after the game," I point out. "Wasn't that support?"

He snorts in derision. "Hardly. He was just covering his own ass."

"For what?" Is this it? Is he referencing this big secret they hold?

"Just making sure I'm keeping my mouth shut."

"About what?" I press into the darkness.

"Let's just get through this surgery. Once I'm on the other side of it, maybe we can revisit this conversation."

I want to push harder. I want to fight for that secret. It's been referenced too many times in my presence, and secrets have this way of coming out one way or another.

But I leave him be.

"So if you're not feeling the fight...what comes next?"

"I guess maybe I set up a meeting with Phil."

I remember meeting the Director of Player Engagement and Development at the Aces facility when Leah took me around to show me the ropes. "Are you leaning one way or another?"

"Maybe coaching," he says dismissively. But then he adds, "I can get a feel for it from the sidelines the rest of this season since I won't be able to suit up."

"I'm so, so sorry, Luke."

He squeezes my hand that's still in his. "I know. Let's get some rest now, okay?"

"Sure. Goodnight."

Neither of us gets any rest, though.

We don't talk, but I toss and turn. Luke is still since he doesn't have much range of movement with his injury, but I can tell he lies awake, too.

When the light of morning dawns, I shift in his direction. His eyes are open as he stares up at the ceiling.

"Six hours until my knee is cut open," he says.

"Good morning to you, too."

He huffs out a little chuckle, and I lean over to kiss his cheek. He turns his head at the last second to catch my lips. "Thanks for our talk last night," he says. "It meant a lot to me to know that you still want to be with me."

My brows dip. "Of course I still want to be with you. I love you, Luke. Broken knee or not."

"I love you, too," he says softly. "Thanks for understanding."

I just pray I can keep understanding as we fight together to get him healthy again.

CHAPTER 5

I stare at the clock on the wall as it seems to move backwards.

I've chewed off every fingernail.

I've been on my phone so much that I killed the battery.

I'm just sitting here now, biding my time in silence as I wait for some news. Any news. I'm desperate to know how he's doing.

The surgery is only supposed to take a few hours. It's been three hours and four minutes.

Nicki and Josh are here with me. It's Josh's day off, thankfully, so at least I don't have to sit here alone. Nobody from Luke's family is here, though.

A doctor walks into the waiting room, and every head in the room swings in his direction as we all wait for updates on our loved ones.

The doctor's eyes land on Josh first and then me beside him. He's an older gentleman with kind brown eyes and graying hair.

"Dr. Charles," Josh says.

He nods at Josh then turns to me. "I assume you're Luke's wife?"

"Yes."

"He's out of surgery. It was a success and I'm confident he'll have full range after physical therapy. He's resting and still under general anesthesia but should be coming out of it any minute. He's in the recovery room and nurses will be moving him to a room for the next two to three days for observation."

"Thank you, Doctor," I say, my voice shaking, and I can't help when I start to weep.

He's okay.

The surgery was a success.

He'll have full range.

I let out a breath.

I feel an arm come around my shoulders, and I turn and cry into my brother's chest. Nicki lightly rubs my back, and I can't help but think what amazing parents these two are going to be.

When I finally compose myself and wipe away the tears, my brother lets out a soft chuckle. "Awfully attached for a fake marriage," he whispers, and I give him a half-smile.

"Not so fake anymore," I say wryly.

A short while later, a nurse pops in to let me know he's awake. "Only the wife can come back to recovery," she says to Josh and Nicki, who sit back down.

I follow her through the surgical recovery room, keeping my eyes on the floor as I feel a little faint. Curtains separate patients knocked out from anesthesia in their beds, and I feel a little queasy as heat creeps up my spine. I've never done well around blood or medical issues in general, so to be back here feels a little terrifying.

The nurse drops me into Luke's bay, and his eyes are closed. Heat presses behind my eyes again as I stare at him. He's pale, and this powerful, strong, lean man who I've seen running on a treadmill so many times looks weak as he lies there. It's not my Luke, but it's my job to help him get back there.

His eyes open and he's groggy as he focuses on me. His lips don't tip into a smile, but his eyes seem to fill with warmth as they land on me. "Hey good lookin'," he croaks. "You come here often?"

I force that dizzy and queasy feeling away as I rush over and press a kiss to his cheek, relieved that the man I fell for is still in there. "How are you feeling?"

"Not great, but this little button that pumps in morphine helps." He indicates a clicker in his hand.

"Can I get one of those?" I tease.

He chuckles. "Doubt it."

He's in better spirits than I would've expected, but he's also high on painkillers.

The nurse comes to transfer him to his room, and she gives me the room number as I take a different route than the medics who wheel Luke's bed through the hallways. I find Josh and Nicki still in the waiting room.

"He's going to be fine," I say, and Josh looks relieved to hear it from me in addition to Dr. Charles. "They're transferring him to a room now. He was even making jokes back there."

"Thank God," Josh murmurs.

They come with me to Luke's room. He's sitting up as a nurse asks him questions while he sips water.

"What's the prognosis, nurse? Is he gonna live?" Josh asks brightly.

She gives him a look like the joke was totally inappropriate, but Luke laughs. It's a relief to hear his laughter again.

"He'll be fine," the nurse says sternly. She glances at her patient. "You need me to kick these jokesters out?"

"Not yet," Luke says.

We all stand around awkwardly for a few beats, and then Josh breaks the silence. "How long will he be in here?"

"Two to three days," she says. "The doctors want to make sure there's no delayed arterial damage."

"When does PT start?" Josh asks, and I'm glad he's here to ask questions since I don't even know where to begin.

"As soon as the swelling goes down and he can stand without significant pain. Two or three weeks probably," she says.

Luke sighs. I'm sure he already knew that, but two or three weeks of sitting around without bearing weight on his knee must sound horrific for someone as active as he is.

Guess it's time to load up on movies and snacks.

The nurse heads out, and Josh and Nicki take off when Luke wants to rest. I sit in a chair in the corner and let him sleep while I look up things to do with someone recovering from surgery. Cards, games, puzzles, discovering new music and movies...there's a list. It's not endless, but we can certainly check off a few things.

I head down to the cafeteria to get some food, and when I get back to his room, Coach Thompson is standing beside Luke asking questions. I'm not sure whether this is a private conversation and I should stay in the hall, but Luke spots me and waves me in.

"Hi, Coach," I say as I move into the room.

"Ellie," he says warmly. "Good to see you again. Luke's been telling me how wonderful you've been, and I can't thank you enough for taking care of my boy."

My boy.

His *coach* is here and his parents aren't. That says something to me. Mitch seems like more of a father to Luke than Tim is. I know the coaching staff at the Aces is fairly new, but clearly these two share a bond.

"I only wish I could do more," I say.

"His smile when he looks at you says it all." He nods briefly at me, like this conversation is getting a little too deep for him, and he turns back to Luke. "I will fight for you with the big guys. You know that, right?"

Luke nods. "I know you will, and I can't tell you how much I appreciate it. I just have no idea whether I'll come back from this."

"You will," Mitch says confidently. "Stronger than ever, kid. Just keep your eye on the ball. Keep your focus, and work hard to get healthy."

After Coach leaves, Luke tells me to go home, but I can't make myself leave.

And so I spend the next two and a half days in a hospital room with my husband.

CHAPTER 6

I texted my mom to let her know that we won't be able to do dinner with Luke just getting out of the hospital. She understands, but I also have an ulterior motive.

I'm not sure I can face my parents without them figuring out I'm pregnant.

I know my mom will be thrilled, and I'm feeling that excitement edge its way in, too, but I'm just not ready to face all this. We agree to a raincheck, and I think Josh was right when he mentioned in passing that he thinks our parents are probably looking at houses here in Vegas. They're both retired, and both their kids live in the same place literally across the street from each other while they're back in Chicago.

The only thing keeping them there is their circle of friends and extended family, but they're out here for most of Josh's home games, so it makes sense for them to make the move.

Josh helps me get Luke into the house, and I've never been more grateful to have my brother literally across the street.

As the doses of morphine decreased over the last couple days, Luke's mood worsened. He's back to lashing out, but I thrive on the little moments when the real him flickers through—though he's trying his best to convince me that *this* is the real him, that this is the guy I've dubbed my Prince Charming.

It's late, and we're both exhausted after sleeping in a hospital for the last few days. We head right to the bedroom we slept in the night before the surgery, and I settle Luke into bed with his leg elevated as the nurse showed me before we left the hospital. I make sure he doesn't need anything before I hop into the shower.

It's glorious.

I take my shower upstairs rather than making noise in the bathroom next to where he's trying to sleep, and when I'm done, I flip through the mail Debbie left on the dresser in the bedroom. No test results just yet. She knew to keep a lookout for the envelope from the LV Paternity Solutions Lab and to text me if it arrived, but I thought maybe she missed it.

Or maybe Michelle got to it first, but we didn't give her a key to the mailbox, so that's doubtful.

Exhaustion hits me, and I head back down to sleep beside Luke just in case he needs anything at all. The room is dark, and I creep quietly to the bed before I slide onto cool sheets beneath a warm comforter.

"I didn't marry Savannah just because I loved her," Luke says quietly into the dark.

I startle at the sound of his voice. I thought he was asleep. "What?" I'm confused. Maybe he's been taking painkillers again and he's confused, too.

"I married her because she knew things and I needed to keep her quiet."

"Quiet about what?" I ask softly.

He sighs. "My parents have been married for thirty-four years, but that doesn't mean they set a good example of what a marriage should look like. The Daltons look a certain way. They always have. But nobody knew how my mother manipulated my father. Nobody knew about the whispered arguments between the two of them that all three of us overheard. Nobody knew that they probably would've been happier apart, but they stuck together. Maybe they really do love each other. There are moments of tenderness there, I guess, but it seems like the bad tends to outweigh the good."

He pauses, and I can't help but wonder how the history of his parents links to why he kept Savannah quiet. But I listen anyway. I wait patiently as he confesses these secrets into the darkness of this room.

I reach over and slide my hand into his. He doesn't move, doesn't flex his fingers, doesn't hold mine back. But I leave mine there anyway, and I tighten my grasp.

"My parents showed me one example, and I followed in their footsteps when Savannah knew things I couldn't afford for anybody else to know."

"What things?" I ask.

He's quiet a beat, but then he starts talking. "When I tore my ACL the first time, I took some drugs Savannah gave me. At the time, we were dating. We were just starting to get serious. Whatever she gave me helped me heal, and nobody could believe how fast my recovery was going. The progress was incredible, and I felt great, so I kept taking them. I increased the dose. I asked her for more, and she gave them to me. And then Jack found the bottle. He confronted me. He told me they were PEDs that were banned by the league. I had no idea they were illegal, but I knew I could get into a hell of a lot of trouble if I was caught."

"What are PEDs?" I ask stupidly.

"Performance enhancing drugs," he says. "I stopped taking them as soon as I learned what they were. Savannah claimed she had no idea they were banned, but she's a sports reporter. She played dumb, and I believed her. She wouldn't have given them to me on purpose if she knew what it could've done to my career. And then a few days later, I was slapped with a random drug test. Hindsight tells me she had something to do with it, but it didn't matter. There was no way I'd pass. PEDs can linger in your system for up to four weeks, so I was fucked."

"What did you do?" My voice is soft in the quiet room.

He clears his throat. "Jack stepped in. He, uh, took the test for me."

"Oh my God, Luke," I gasp. "Isn't that illegal?"

"Very. It's considered fraud. But he did it to protect me. He confessed to my parents when my test showed up clean, and that's when I was pushed aside as the family outcast. The fact that I let my brother put himself at risk when he was a rising star was unacceptable to them."

"Does Kaylee know?"

"No," he says quietly. "My parents. Jack. Me. Savannah. And now you. That's it."

"I don't get it," I say stupidly. "Why did she do it?"

"My guess is so that she'd have something over me. Insurance, if you will. She's a master manipulator, and looking back now, I know she only married me for money. She divorced me knowing she'd get more out of me with the evidence she held."

"Why are you telling me?" I ask, truly curious as to what his answer might be.

"Because you've shown me what a real marriage looks like." He's quiet a beat. "You've been there for me in ways nobody else has ever before in my entire life."

"So why did you marry her if you didn't trust her?"

"She'd been pushing for a ring, though I'm not totally sure she cared if it was from me or my brother. I think she gave me those drugs so I'd be dependent on her, regardless of whether she knew what she was giving me." He lowers his voice. "I did love her even though I didn't fully trust her, but I looked to my parents for the example. They didn't trust each other, either. I was young and dumb, and I thought I needed to marry her to keep her loyal."

"And you divorced her..." I prod.

"When I could no longer take being manipulated by her." He doesn't mask the hostility in his tone. "I did what my father never could when it came to my mother. Savannah just wanted money and the last name of an NFL star to seal her career as a sports reporter. To make it look like she had the inside track, which she did. For years. She had total inside access first to my brother and then to me. She got to see the inner workings of three different teams. She got to see inside the heads of two players in different positions, including one who was traded while they were together. And she made out with plenty of cash."

"What would happen if the truth came out now?" I ask.

"The league would open an investigation, I suppose," he says. "There could be fines or suspensions or even worse."

"How would a suspension work with you being injured?" I ask.

"I don't really know. It would depend how the news came out. If it was public, the punishment would be harsher. If it's within the organization, it would probably just be swept away like everything else."

"What's the suspension for something like that?" I ask.

"First time offense for substituting a specimen would be two weeks for Jack. For attempting to substitute a specimen *and* having evidence of the drugs, which Savannah has, it'd be six weeks for me. But those are penalties for guys currently doping, not who did something eight years ago. I don't even know if there's a statute of limitations on something like that."

"Did it happen in Nevada?" I ask.

"Yeah."

I grab my phone and look it up. "The statute of limitations for fraud in this state is four years." I click off my phone and set it back on the nightstand.

"Well at least we're clear legally then."

He yawns. I can't see it in the dark, but I can hear it. "Get some rest. We'll talk more tomorrow," I say, though I'm not sure why I'm ending this conversation when he's finally telling me everything I've been wanting to know.

"Okay," he says.

"Thanks for letting me in," I say, settling my hand back into his. "Thanks for trusting me with your secrets."

"Thanks for being someone I can trust." He flexes his fingers in mine, and then his breathing evens out as he falls asleep.

My mind is buzzing now, though. I can't just go to sleep after that confession.

What if the truth comes out? Savannah knows, and she wasn't the nicest person when I met her. She can't be happy that Luke knocked up one woman and married another and she no longer holds his attention. She might even be worried about the money he pays her.

We need to find a way to make sure she keeps this story to herself. I know it's been eight years, but my gut tells me she's just waiting for the right moment.

I can't let her kick Luke when he's already down.

CHAPTER 7

I'm tired when I "wake up" in the morning, and I use that term loosely since in order to wake up, you're supposed to fall asleep at some point. Dawn is just starting to light up the room.

Between Luke moving and shifting all night as he tried to find a comfortable sleeping position and my mind reeling at his midnight confessions in the dark, I couldn't find a way to calm my thoughts enough to actually sleep.

I need a plan.

I need pre-damage control.

But I also need to let Luke's loyal fanbase know that he's okay. I haven't posted anything yet. I've been waiting for him to be in the right mood to give me a statement, and that hasn't happened just yet.

I'm still shocked he confessed his little story last night, to be honest. Maybe it's the painkillers or maybe it's the fact that I didn't run just because he's hurt.

I turn over and find that Luke's awake, too. He's staring blankly up at the ceiling.

"Did you get any rest?" I ask.

"No." He doesn't move his gaze from the ceiling, and I can't help but look up there, too. I don't see anything. "You?" he asks.

"Nope."

"Sleep upstairs tonight," he says. "You shouldn't miss out on sleep because of me, and I can call you if I need anything."

"You *can*," I say. "But you won't."

He shifts a little then winces.

"How's it feeling?" I ask, sitting up and nodding toward his knee.

"Like hell."

"I'm sorry. Want me to get you some pain meds?"

He blows out a breath. "I'm trying to do this without them given what happened last time. But not taking them will make me crabby."

I narrow my eyes at him. "Who, you?"

He lets off a soft chuckle.

"You've been crabby since the morning after I met you. Maybe even that night."

His brows dip. "I was *not* crabby the night we met," he says crossly.

"You whipped out a stack of condoms that were enough to nearly scare me away and you complained about how your buddies had been ribbing you all night about it having been too long since you had sex. You were *totally* crabby."

"Whatever," he mutters.

I giggle. "See? Crabby. Let me make you breakfast. Or give you some morning sex?"

It's his turn to narrow his eyes at me. "You know I can't have sex."

"Why not?"

He rolls his eyes. "How do I thrust when I can't use my knees?"

Heat crawls up my neck as I think about him thrusting. "You let me do all the work," I say, though to be honest I'm a little scared of bumping his knee the wrong way.

"Let's give it another day or two. But I will take you up on the breakfast offer. Can you just help me out of bed?"

I don't feel quite as rejected as the other day in the shower. That's something, at least.

We make it to the kitchen and I help Luke settle into a chair at the table. I set another chair across from him to prop his leg up. "Do your stretches," I say. He has a whole list of things he's supposed to do four times a day to help rehab his knee. I set to work on the task of making breakfast, glancing up at him every few minutes to check that he's doing his exercises.

He isn't.

I want to badger him about it.

I don't.

I set scrambled eggs, toast, and bacon on plates for us and join him at the table.

"This is going to sound weird, but I feel closer to you after our talk last night," I say. I dive into the scrambled eggs. I might not be the best chef in the world, but I do make a mean egg.

"Not weird at all," he says. "And I feel the same."

I want to ask more. I want to expand on that.

But Michelle still lives here, and she's the last person we'd want finding out about Luke's past. I get why the brothers are so careful with their secret. If it ever came out, it wouldn't just make them look bad. It would make their teams look bad...maybe even the entire organization.

The doorbell rings, and I head over to answer it. The mailman stands there with an envelope marked *Certified Mail.* "Is Luke Dalton home?" he asks.

"He is," I say. "He can't come to the door. Would you like to come in?"

He looks a little uncertain.

"He just had surgery and can't walk," I explain. "I can bring you to him in the kitchen."

He nods. "Fine."

I try to get a good look at the envelope but I can't see who it's from. It *has* to be the test results. I didn't realize they'd come certified, so it's a good thing Luke is home from the hospital.

My heart races. My chest tightens. My stomach turns, and I very nearly catch myself resting a hand on my lower belly.

This is it. The moment of truth. Either Luke Dalton is going to father two children a couple months apart or potentially just one pending my doctor's appointment on Thursday.

I show the mailman out and when I return to the kitchen, Luke is eating his eggs while the envelope rests beside him on the table. He's staring at it.

"You ready to open it?" I ask.

He shrugs but doesn't say anything. How can he sit there so casually when in many ways, the fate of the rest of his life lies inside that envelope? This will tell him whether he can kick out the toxic woman trying to suck the life out of him...or it'll tell him he'll be co-parenting with her.

"You need me to?" I press.

His eyes lock on mine. "There's just a lot riding on what's inside that envelope, and I'm not sure I'm in a place to handle any more upheaval."

I reach across the table and squeeze his hand as my heart pounds loudly in my chest. He doesn't want any more upheaval...but I've got my own little secret that will send both of us into a tailspin once it's confirmed. At least it'll be a *happy* tailspin. I think. "I get that. But you know what? Regardless of what the paper in there says, either things stay the same or they get easier. Right?"

He nods, and then he shoves the envelope toward me. "You do it."

I don't hesitate. I tear open the envelope and pull out a small stack of papers.

I scan the top page, a little note thanking us for using their lab. I flip to the next page, where I see a chart with a bunch of numbers on it. I spot Luke's name at the top, and then at the bottom I read the statement to myself.

My head buzzes as the results register, and then I read it aloud to Luke. "Based on an analysis of the STR loci listed above, the probability of paternity is seventeen-point-three-three-three percent."

Luke's brows dip. "Seventeen percent?" he asks. "But that would mean..."

"You share *some* DNA with the child, but not enough to conclusively state that you're the father."

Our eyes meet across the table and mine widen as I realize what this means.

"Jack," he hisses.

CHAPTER 8

I clutch the paper as I stand from the table, anger permeating my veins and seeping into my bloodstream. How could she do this to him? And *why* would she do this to him?

I stalk furiously through the kitchen so I can go to her room and give her a piece of my damn mind when Luke's voice stops me. "Wait."

I halt in place and turn around.

"Let me handle this."

"I was about to head to her room to kick her the hell out of here," I say.

"I know exactly what you were about to do," he says thinly, "and this is *my* problem to handle. I don't need you tackling it for me."

"It's *our* problem," I remind him as hurt stabs at me that he wants to do this alone when we've been in it together the entire time, all the way back to when I first saw the headline when I woke up one morning and was the one who told him he was having a baby with her as he was dripping with sweat from running on the treadmill.

God, those were such simpler times.

I set my hand on my hip. "Fine. Want me to go get her?"

"She'll slither out eventually. Until then, I plan to enjoy my eggs in peace knowing that I didn't make the biggest mistake of my life." He holds up his glass of orange juice like he's about to make a toast. "Dodged a bullet there."

I hope he's talking about sleeping with Michelle and not about having children in general.

"Aren't you mad?" I ask, walking back to the table to sit. I push my plate aside. It's not like I can enjoy my half-eaten breakfast now that I have this information.

He nods. "Furious. But she's still my boss's daughter. I can't have you making things worse."

"That's not what I was going to do!" I protest.

"Oh, come on, Ellie. Yes it was. You were going to go kick her out of the house with *joy*."

He's not wrong there.

"Look, I've got enough problems. I don't need you making one more."

I glare across the table at him. "Fine. Enjoy your breakfast." I stalk out of the room and head to my office to pout there.

Maybe I'm being mean. He'll need help when he's done eating. He can't get from the table to anywhere else, especially not with how far out of his reach I stored his crutches once he was in position at the table—not to be mean, but just to get them out of the way.

I'm sure Michelle will come along to help.

I hate my bitter thoughts where she's concerned, but I can't help it. I want her out. Now. She's provided enough distraction for Luke. Maybe if none of this had ever happened, he wouldn't have gotten hurt. I realize that's a real stretch since it was the fault of another player doing something dirty, but maybe he would've seen it coming if he hadn't been distracted, if he would've had just a little more focus instead of being pulled in a million directions in his personal life between his family and Michelle.

And me, I suppose.

I heave out a breath.

I can't get mad at him for wanting to handle things his own way. I've heard of pregnancy hormones before, and maybe this little spat is my first real experience with them.

I draft up a statement to post on his social media, and after a while I head back to the kitchen to show it to him and get his final approval before posting. He hasn't asked for approval since my first few posts, but I feel like this is one he'll want a little control over.

He doesn't apologize for his comments when I slide into the chair across from him, but I guess I didn't really expect him to. Instead, I let it tug at my thoughts. Letting these things build without confronting him is going to get ugly, but he's recovering from major knee surgery along with the devastating loss of his football season—and potentially his entire career. I'll give him a pass on a stupid comment that I'm sure he didn't even mean.

"I drafted up a little thing to post to let your fans know you're okay," I say, and I shove the paper in front of him.

He glances over it, and before he gets a chance to respond to my hard work, Michelle waltzes in. "Good morning, everyone," she says brightly. She has no idea what we know.

"Morning," Luke mutters. I glance around the table and don't see the envelope with the test results. How'd he do that? He couldn't have gotten up from his chair. He must be fucking Houdini. My gaze finally lands on his, and he shakes his head just slightly to remind me to keep my mouth shut.

"Good morning," I say sweetly. The last *good morning* you'll be spending here, you evil bitch.

She sets about making herself a bowl of yogurt with some berries, and then she joins us at the table. "How's the knee, big man?" she asks.

Big man? Is that some pet nickname I never knew about? Gag me.

"Hurts. Where were you on March thirty-first?" he asks without preamble.

Her eyes dart from her yogurt to him and back again to her bowl. She looks guilty. "I don't remember, Luke. That was almost six months ago."

He narrows his eyes. "Stop acting like you don't know. Tell the goddamn truth for once."

Her brows dip. "What, exactly, are you accusing me of now?"

Luke blows out a breath. "You know, I thought it was strange when you showed up in Hawaii with my brother. Even stranger that you were *so adamant* that this is my baby. But the strangest thing of all is that there's no way I was so drunk on the night of April fifth that I would've had sex with you, especially not when I was so angry with you after we broke up. So you either need to tell the truth about that night we were together, or you need to tell the truth about who else you were with at the end of March."

"I, uh..." she stutters and stammers a bit. "You and I were together, Luke."

He shakes his head. "You know, the more I think about it, the more convinced I become that we weren't. What I think happened, and you feel free to correct any details I might get wrong here, is that you were with someone else, had a feeling you might've gotten knocked up, and decided to use that to try to get me back. You came here that night, and you slipped me something that made me pass out because I sure as hell wasn't drunk enough to fuck you. Then you found a way for us to wake up naked together and you left me to make assumptions."

Her jaw drops. "How could you even say that to me?"

He pulls the papers from his lap where apparently he's been hiding them. "Because these DNA results show that there's only a seventeen percent chance I'm your baby's father, which tells me that either you and I are related or you fucked someone in my family."

Her eyes widen as she realizes for the first time that she's caught.

A sense of vindication washes over me.

"You might want to have Jack's DNA tested," he says. "And since I can't throw these papers at you before I storm out of the room thanks to my fucked-up knee, you can see yourself out. Oh, and move the hell out of my house by the end of the day."

She stares across the table at him, and then she looks at me. "It's her, isn't it? She did this. She turned you into this monster I don't even recognize."

"No, Michelle," he says. "That was all you."

"My dad will be hearing about this," she says, standing up as she tosses her spoon down on the table.

Real classy, Michelle. Use your damn father against a man whose career might be over anyway.

"You do that," Luke says, his voice escalating. "You make sure to tell him how you used me, lied to me, and manipulated me. I guarantee I won't be the one to come out of that looking like the asshole you'll try your hardest to paint me as."

She glares at him. "Your career is over. I'll make sure of it."

"You have no power," he says dismissively. He's not scared of her threats, and I've never been prouder of him. He shifts in his chair and winces at the movement. He hasn't had his pain pills yet this morning, and he probably needs them even more after this conversation with Michelle.

"Get out," I say to her through a clenched jaw. "Luke needs a calm home to recover in, and you're not welcome here in it."

The look she gives us both tells me this isn't the last we've seen of her before she spins on her heel and stalks out of the room.

"I hear Denver's real nice in the winter," Luke calls after her retreating figure.

If our suspicions are true and Jack is actually the one who knocked her up, then she'll still be part of Luke's extended family. But who knows what that even means at this point—it could very well mean that he *might* see his niece or nephew once a year, or maybe not. Maybe he doesn't want anything at all to do with his family anymore—especially not when Jack went behind his back and helped Michelle keep up the lie.

"You okay?" I ask, nodding toward the hallway she just disappeared down.

"Fine," he mutters.

"I just mean about the news."

"I know what you meant," he says shortly. "And it's fine."

Few things are more unconvincing than his tone, but I let it go.

Seems I'm doing a lot of that lately. I'm starting to wonder how many things I should let go before it's one too many.

CHAPTER 9

I'm in the kitchen cleaning up our breakfast dishes less than an hour later when Michelle comes slithering back in. "Can we talk?"

I helped Luke move to the couch a little while ago, and he's still angry. Now isn't the time, but I guess she thinks an hour is enough for him to cool down. Maybe I know him better than she does, because I know it's not nearly long enough. Forever might not even be long enough to forgive what she did.

"About what?" Luke grunts, and it's nice to have his moodiness directed at someone other than me.

She stands in front of him with her arms crossed over her chest, and it's maybe the most vulnerable I've ever seen her. But it's still fake. It's a game, and that's all any of this ever was to her, which is a real shame considering there's a baby involved.

She glances over at me, and then she lowers her voice—but not so low I can't still hear her (maybe since I'm literally hanging onto every word she speaks). "I'm sorry. I just so badly wanted it to be yours. I wanted a life with you."

"And you thought trapping me with a baby was the way to do that? That's really fucked up, Michelle. Even for you."

She starts crying, but I can't muster any sympathy for her. I doubt Luke will, either.

"What I did with Jack...it was a mistake." She sniffles and seems to tighten her arms around herself. "I know that now. I just thought you'd fight for me."

"You played a game, and you lost," he says flatly. "After what happened with Savannah, you should've known better. And I don't really care what you and Jack did. I'm just glad I'm not going to be tied to you for the rest of my life."

There's a knock at the front door, and I move to answer it.

When I open it, I'm shocked at who's standing on the other side. "Calvin," I whisper.

His lips thin. "May I come in?"

"Of course." I open the door wider and I lead the way to the family room where my husband and his daughter are currently duking it out. Or as Michelle stands there looking all apologetic and Luke lies helplessly on the couch.

"Daddy!" Michelle says when she sees him, and she rushes toward him. He pats her back gently as he gives her a hug.

"Mr. Bennett," Luke says, sitting up a little straighter.

"How's the knee?" Calvin grunts.

Luke clears his throat. "Fresh off surgery that was a total success. Dr. Charles says I'll get complete range of motion back with a little PT."

Well that's certainly a more optimistic picture than he's been painting for everyone else.

"Glad to hear it," he says. "I came to help Michelle get her stuff out of here. She'll be coming home with me a while."

Does that mean he knows the truth? Did Michelle actually confess to her father that she's a manipulating bitch who slept with brothers just to make one of them jealous?

If he wasn't standing here in my family room, I wouldn't believe it.

An awkward beat of silence passes, and then Calvin gives Michelle a stern look before he glances at Luke. "I'm sorry for what she's put you through." His voice is gruff, and Michelle looks absolutely miserable. She didn't just lose Luke. She also disappointed her father.

A moving truck comes by later in the afternoon, and Calvin takes off with very little interaction aside from when he first walked in.

And that's it. Michelle is out. She's gone, and that's all I care about.

* * *

Luke is propped on the couch with pillows elevating his knee on Sunday at ten when the first game starts in our time zone.

The Aces are playing at home, which apparently means the afternoon game, and I guess it also means it's Football Sunday just as it's been my entire life.

At least I sort of understand the game now, though not watching Luke strut around in those tight little football pants will definitely make it a whole lot more boring.

We watch the Broncos game first, and he watches both his brother and Allen Hammond, who's back on the field like nothing happened last Sunday. It reminds me that today is the first Sunday Luke doesn't get to play, and the thought makes me sad. He won't get to play for the entire rest of the season. The Aces are projected to do really well. This season could be his shot at a Super Bowl ring, and while I believe he'll still get one if the team wins the big game, this certainly wouldn't be how he'd want it. Maybe they won't even get there with one of their key players out.

My heart breaks for him.

Luke studies every play. I set a bowl of popcorn beside him, but it sits totally neglected as he pauses and rewinds live TV so he can focus on what certain players are doing and then watch again to see what other players are doing in reaction.

It's not really the most entertaining way to watch the game, but it does tell me he'd make a good position coach. I still want to get him to talk about the future, but he's so focused on his injury right now that it's just not a good time.

I head to my office. Two of the Aces guys have signed up for publicity with me and both are looking for community outreach ideas, so I research some different opportunities that take place on Tuesdays since that's their only day off.

I drown myself in work for a couple hours, and then I grab lunch for both Luke and me around noon. I set a sandwich and salad on the couch beside him, and he hardly acknowledges me.

I go back to the office, and when I emerge at one to watch the Aces game with him, I see that his sandwich and salad still sit untouched beside him.

"Eat," I command.

He doesn't even look at me. "Not hungry," he grunts.

"Eat it anyway, or Pepper will." I go for a light, teasing tone.

He pushes the plate away.

"Come on, Luke," I beg. "You need your strength to get healthy. At least do your leg exercises if you won't eat."

He sighs. "What difference does it make? We both know this is the end of my career."

"Regardless of what comes next in your career, you're young. You still need to get healthy. Are you just going to sit on the couch with your knee propped for the rest of your life?"

He purses his lips, and I wonder what he'd do without me. Maybe sit on the couch forever.

I'm not allowing that.

"I know it's a tough road." I take his hand in mine. "But I'm right here, okay?" I know it's not enough, that *I* am not enough, but I still need him to know he isn't going through this alone. And when I say that I'm right here, I really mean we—both me and this baby I think I'm carrying. "We'll get through it. You'll come out stronger once you're able to start therapy."

He pulls his hand away. "You and I both know that's not true."

I pick up his plate and set it directly on his lap. "I know it's true. I just need you to believe it, too. Having a bad attitude isn't going to change it."

He lets out an exaggerated sigh, like I'm an annoyance who's just in his way. And then the Aces game starts, and that's the end of our conversation as he laser-focuses on it.

"Coach put in Higgins," he mutters as soon as he sees his team take the field. "I knew he would. That kid was just waiting for something to happen to either Josh or me. Man, did he luck the fuck out."

"You getting hurt isn't lucky for anybody," I say, doing my best to keep the tone positive in here.

He just gives me a look like I'm dumb. Maybe I am for believing the best in people, but I guess it's true. Tristan Higgins wouldn't have gotten this opportunity today if Luke was on the field.

I sit beside him as we watch a little bit of the game, and he yells at the television. A lot. I've never seen him get so passionate about anything before, and if we weren't sitting here because he's hurt, it would be hilariously entertaining to watch him.

But the truth of the matter is that we *are* here because of an injury.

Higgins makes some unbelievable catch, and Luke mutters a curse.

"Why's it a bad thing he made that catch?" I ask.

He gives me that same look as before, and then he sighs. "This is his chance to prove he's more valuable than me, and he's doing it. Handily. They won't negotiate a new contract with me because they won't need me anymore." He shakes his head and keeps his eyes focused on the screen.

"Not even as a back-up?" I ask. I don't know how this works.

"They're not gonna pay me to be a back-up."

"But someone else might," I point out.

He lifts a shoulder. "Yeah." He's made it clear before that he doesn't want to play somewhere else. He wants to stay with the Aces. But from what I've learned from the other football wives, these men don't really get much of a say in it. It's a business, and transactions are made based on that fact.

"I wish I could fucking be there today," he says. He glares down at his knee as if that'll change things. It doesn't.

"Do you still *want* to play?" I ask.

I get the look. Again.

"Then eat your damn sandwich," I scold.

He flattens his lips and his nostrils flare, but then, miraculously, he picks it up and takes a bite.

I don't want to treat him like a child, but if he's going to act like one, then I will.

After all, now's as good a time as any to start learning how to deal with children since I might have one of my own soon.

CHAPTER 10

The road to Thursday is long.

I'm nervous about my doctor appointment, and I'm keeping it close to the vest so I don't even have anyone to talk to about it. I almost slip to Nicki when she talks about how she's nearly at the second trimester, which is supposed to be much smoother sailing than the first, but I manage to cover it up.

I almost slip again when Josh asks if I want a glass of wine one night when they come over for dinner. I tell him I'm not drinking in solidarity with Luke, who isn't supposed to be mixing alcohol with painkillers.

With Michelle out of the house, we can rest easy knowing any conversations we have are safe—provided she didn't plant a bug, which I wouldn't put past her.

Still, though, with everything going on, I feel like it's best to just keep quiet about it until it's confirmed by a doctor and not a drugstore test.

It's Wednesday night before I finally get Luke to talk.

He just took his pain meds, and he's in a better mood than he has been the last couple days as I've let more and more slide when it comes to the way he treats me. I often think back on Josh's words not to take any shit from Luke, and I'm afraid it's too late. On the other hand, I also think back on Luke's words to be patient with him. I know the man I fell in love with is in there underneath this grumpy exterior, and I'll get him back. He just needs a little TLC.

"You haven't really talked about how you're feeling about the fact that Michelle's baby isn't yours," I begin as we sit down to Debbie's world-famous shredded chicken tacos.

He grunts and takes a bite of his taco, and I wait patiently for his answer. I stare across the table at him with raised brows, and when he glances up and catches my eye, he sighs.

I know he doesn't want to have this conversation, but it's important to me. I need to know where he stands on having kids in general. He mentioned to me that he wants kids with me sometime down the road...but that was before the injury.

"Relieved," he finally says.

That was sort of my fear, but before I read too much into his answer, I get him to clarify. "Why?"

He clears his throat and looks past me out the window. "You know I want kids someday down the line, but I never wanted them with her. I guess I'm just relieved I won't be tied to her for the rest of my life." He shakes his head and his eyes move to mine. "In some ways I will be if it's really Jack's, but at least she won't be *my* problem. You know?"

I nod, satisfied with that answer. Until he continues.

"But it's not just that. Right now...it's not just bad timing. I've got rehab. I've got a long road ahead of me. I don't know what next year will look like, or even beyond that. I need a stable future before I can even begin to think about kids. And I need to be selfish to get healthy. Worrying about her pregnancy and delivery and then having a newborn, it's all just too much. But it's Jack's problem now."

I press my lips together and force any emotions tightening my chest away.

I get what he's saying, but he's saying these words a little preemptively. And now I'm even more terrified to go to this appointment tomorrow. When I get the official confirmation and due date and it all becomes real instead of some abstract idea...then what?

How do I tell him?

I clear my throat. "Jack's problem?" I repeat. "Has he taken the test?"

Luke nods. "Confirmed. It's his. Ninety-nine percent match."

"How'd you find out?" My brows dip.

"He texted me this morning."

"I didn't know you two texted." I take a bite of taco.

"Well we do. I guess there's a lot you don't know about me." He says it like he's musing, but it's true—and it cuts deeper than it should.

* * *

I pre-filled out the paperwork online, so when I arrive for my appointment, all I have to do after I check in is leave a urine sample then sit and wait for my name to be called.

The urine sample thing sounds pretty self-explanatory, right?

It's not. Nobody really tells you what to do, and in true Ellie *falling into the pool at my brother's wedding* fashion, I have no idea how to do this.

I'm nervous and anxious about this appointment, particularly after Luke's words last night, so I'm distracted. And distracted Ellie is never a good thing.

I hover over a cup and do my best work, filling it about a quarter inch. I hope that's enough because I didn't know I was going to have to do this and the tank is empty.

I set the cup on the floor once I'm done so I can pull up my pants, and when I move to flush, I kick it over on accident.

My quarter inch spills all over my shoes.

I gasp as I stare at the floor, and then I heave out a heavy sigh as I try to clean up both my shoes and the floor with some combination of toilet paper and paper towels. The floor is mostly dry, but it smells like ammonia in here.

I chug some sink water, which nearly makes me gag, and force out another sixteenth of an inch, careful not to knock it over this time.

And the best part? I get to tell the lady at the front desk the bathroom floor needs some disinfecting.

As my brother would say...*only you, Ellie.*

Once I'm back in the waiting room and nobody sits by me because my shoes smell, the ultrasound technician calls me in.

I sit on the table just as I saw Michelle do not so long ago, and the tech squirts the same jelly on my stomach. She moves it around with her magic wand, and I see a bunch of lines on the screen.

Then I hear a *whoosh-whoosh-whoosh* sound.

"There's the heartbeat," she says.

Tears spring to my eyes. *Whoosh-whoosh-whoosh.*

This is the first time this has actually felt real since I took that test. I know it said positive, but when you don't really feel any different and you can't see inside there, it's sort of hard to believe, or it's easier to believe it's a false positive.

But this right here is hard evidence.

She takes some measurements. "You're measuring at seven weeks, four days."

"Seven weeks?" I blurt. "I've been pregnant for *seven weeks?*"

She nods and smiles. She must hear exclamations like that all the time.

"Everything looks great." She prints out some pictures and hands them over to me. I stare at the wavy lines. One of them has the word *baby* with an arrow pointing down to what looks like a little jellybean.

My little jellybean.

"You can head back to the waiting room and your doctor will call you in shortly," she says, and I'm just supposed to get up and walk into the waiting room?

But I'm pregnant! Is that safe?

Okay, I'm being dramatic. But the point is that I have no idea what this means. I have no idea how to take care of a pregnant body. I wasn't real sure how to take care of a regular body, either. Or shoes, apparently.

And I express that as soon as I'm called back. The tech takes my blood pressure and records some things on a sheet of paper. "Congratulations," she says.

"Thanks. So what do I do?" I ask.

"What do you mean?"

"How do I take care of myself?" I ask, or rather, I beg. "How do I keep this baby safe?"

She smiles. "The doctor will have all sorts of information for you as well as resources to help you. But during my first pregnancy, I asked my sister *everything*. She had two kids. Do you have someone like that you can go to?"

Nicki pops immediately to mind. "My best friend is pregnant."

"Aw, you two can go through this together. So sweet."

I smile. She's right. It'll be a lifesaver—or at least a sanity saver—to have her nearby.

The doctor comes in, and the tech was right. She gives me an entire bag of stuff for newly pregnant mothers (*mothers!* I'm going to be someone's *mother*), and I'm going to need to find somewhere to put this until I figure out a way to tell Luke about this little secret.

She gives me a quick exam and taps some stuff onto a tablet. Before she leaves, she asks if I have any questions.

There's one question that keeps flitting through my mind. I guess this is my chance to ask it. "I've been on the pill for years. How did this happen?"

"There are lots of potential reasons," she says, sitting on a stool to explain. "The pill is ninety-nine percent effective when it's taken perfectly. For most women, that's a little closer to about ninety-one percent, and lots of things can affect it. For example, if you take it at different times, or if you miss one, or even if you drink too much or take certain medications. Do any of those sound relatable?"

"Possibly the drinking thing," I admit. And there may have been a day or two where I took it later than usual or when I missed it altogether. It's all sort of running together now, and for the first time, I'm starting to feel a little queasy.

"And you're aware of all your options?"

I nod. We all learned of the options back in our high school health classes, right? And regardless of how this happened, I feel a sudden fierce protection over whatever's growing in there. Something I've never felt before in my life tugs at my conscience, something that tells me I will stop at nothing to ensure this baby is safe, protected, and loved.

"How soon can I find out gender?" I ask. It's a boy. I can feel it.

"Usually around twenty weeks, but if you decide to get the genetic testing done, that can be done as early as ten weeks and it screens for gender with ninety-nine percent accuracy."

My brows dip. "What's the genetic testing?"

"A noninvasive prenatal test that screens for certain genetic disorders," she explains.

"Am I supposed to get that done?" I ask.

"That's a decision for you and the father, if you're including him in the decision-making."

"I am," I say quickly. "I just have to figure out how to tell him we're having a baby."

She smiles. "Are you going to do something special?"

"I don't know," I murmur.

"Read through the new mom packet in the bag I gave you, and feel free to call the office at any time with any questions," she says. "We'll see you back in a month, or if you want the genetic testing, a bit sooner."

I nod, and she leaves.

I make my next appointment for a month. Once I figure out how to tell Luke, we can discuss the genetic testing.

Holy shit.

I'm having a baby.

With someone who counted his blessings just the other day that he's *not* having one.

CHAPTER 11

"I'm pregnant."

I say it into the mirror, and it still doesn't feel real. Now that it's confirmed, I should tell Luke. I just have no idea how to break this news to someone whose entire life is already in complete upheaval. This will throw him into a tailspin, and somehow I can't help feeling like it's my fault. I realize it took two of us to create this life, but I assured him I was on the pill. I thought we were safe. I even urged him to forego the condom.

And despite this totally unplanned surprise, that's exactly what it is—a surprise. It's not a mistake. It's not a problem. It's not an accident.

It's a baby.

A baby that's part me and part the man I love, and when we said our vows that we'd join together in all that is to come, well...this is part of it. Our vows were real even though our intent wasn't.

I just hope he'll feel the same.

I don't have a plan other than to just go down there and blurt it out.

But when I get to the family room, he's still engrossed in football. Instead, I take Pepper outside. We sit on the patio for a little while, and I confess my secret to her. Her ears perk up. Her life's about to change, too, and the pup doesn't even know it.

I lose my nerve. Friday morning means a doctor appointment for Luke at the Aces' practice facility, where a team doctor talks to him about his progress.

"Have you been doing the stretches they gave you at the hospital?" he asks.

Luke nods, but I jump in with the accurate information. "Not as often as he's supposed to."

Luke glares at me for telling the truth, but I don't care. Go ahead and get mad at me, dude. This is about recovery, not about pretending to be an angel.

"The swelling is much better," the doctor says, "but since you still can't bear weight without pain, we'll hold off another week on physical therapy. Potentially next week, but possibly a little longer yet. No walking and no bearing weight until you see me next Monday, but you *need* to do the stretches. You won't be ready for PT if you don't start rebuilding the muscles and movement. Understand?"

Luke is obviously disappointed, but he nods.

"Coach will be in shortly," the doctor says, and he leaves.

"Thanks for ratting me out," he snarls at me once the door clicks shut behind the doctor.

I just smile sweetly.

Coach Thompson knocks on the door and lets himself in. His eyes edge over to me before they land on Luke again. "Can we talk?"

Luke glances at me and then at him again. "Yeah." He nods and doesn't dismiss me from the room, and for some reason my heart lifts a little at that. He trusts me enough to be in here while this conversation happens, whatever it might entail—and that means something to me.

Coach blows out a breath. "Cal was breathing down my neck about next year before your injury, but about a week ago, he seemed to let up a little. Any idea why?"

"Michelle's baby isn't mine," he admits.

"Thank God for that," Coach mutters, and I stifle a laugh. "What do you want next year? This is you and me, kid. Be honest."

"I want my fucking knee back," Luke says.

"Then you gotta work for it," he says, and I hope his words get through to Luke. If they don't, I'm afraid Luke will fall into a pit of despair where he won't bother taking care of himself because he doesn't see any reason why he should.

I have a reason.

"What else?" Coach asks.

"I want to play."

"Another thing you gotta work for. I hate to break it to you, but that Higgins boy is *fast*. You need to keep up with him despite the bum knee or you need to take out Nolan." My eyes lift to Coach's at the mention of my brother. "I know that's not an option. But might I remind you that as much as we're a family, we're still cutthroat, Luke. It's still every man for himself out on that field, and I don't know whether the man upstairs is issuing a contract to an injured player who's been in the league nine years already."

"But I put up record numbers last season," Luke protests. This is his shot to plead his case, and clearly he's jumping at it. "If this injury hadn't sidelined me, I would've done it again. You have to fight for me, Coach. I need you."

Coach presses his lips together. "You know how I feel about you, Luke." His voice is gruff. "You're a son to me. I'll do what I can, but I can't make any guarantees."

"That's all I'm asking," Luke says.

"How's the progress?" Coach asks, nodding to Luke's knee.

Luke's eyes move to his knee, too. "Doc said the swelling has gone down but I can't start PT until next week at the earliest."

"Then you sit on your ass until you're able to start PT, and you put in the work to get better," Coach says. "It's the only way you've got even a half a shot at coming back next year."

Luke nods. "Understood."

Coach blows out a breath. "We miss you, Luke. The locker room isn't the same without you."

"You just miss the granola bars," Luke says, and Coach laughs. "I'll have Deb whip up a batch."

Coach claps him on the shoulder. "I'm sorry this happened to you. It's the shit end of the stick. But get well soon, kid. We need you back."

"Thanks," Luke says, and he seems a little emotional at his coach's words.

Josh is waiting for us when Coach leaves, and he helps Luke from the exam table and into a wheelchair. And then we head home—all three of us, which makes telling Luke about the baby a little more difficult.

I guess I'll just put it off a little longer.

CHAPTER 12

"What are these granola bars Luke mentioned to Coach Thompson?" I ask Debbie on Saturday morning.

She chuckles. "I make these homemade granola bars and the boys all go crazy for them. Luke brings them in every Thursday since that's their hardest day of practice."

"Can you make some for Luke?" I ask. "I think they'd really cheer him up. And I want to try them too."

Debbie laughs. "Of course, dear." She lowers her voice and nods toward the family room, where Luke is watching—surprise, surprise—football again. He's far enough away and engrossed enough in the game that he can't hear us. "How's he doing?"

I lift a shoulder. "Good days and bad. More bad. Mostly I just try to be helpful and kind of stay out of his way."

"Is he being nice to you?"

I laugh at the question, but it isn't long before I get sort of serious. "No, not really."

"That's how he was the last time he was hurt, too. He was extra grumpy with Savannah, though he was always sort of grumpy with her."

"So what do I do?" I ask.

"You put him in his place. I've known Luke a lot of years, and I know he loves you. You can't let him walk all over you. That's not the strong woman he fell in love with, is it?"

I shake my head sadly. "No, it isn't."

"He'll never tell you when he needs anything. He's too hard-headed. So you just have to do your best to read his mind." She winks at me, and I giggle.

"There's just so much on his plate that I don't blame him for being a little grumpy."

She nods. "But no matter how much is on his plate, that doesn't give him a right to take it out on you."

"True," I concede, and I have the sudden urge to confess my little secret to her. "Can I tell you something that stays between us?" I ask, lowering my voice.

"Of course you can."

I glance at Luke. He's still watching the game. I glance back at Debbie.

"Oh," she says, her mouth dropping open. She covers it. "You're not..." She nods toward my belly with wide eyes.

I nod, and I can't believe the amount of relief that flits through me at *finally* unloading this very big secret on someone. I'll never know why it's Debbie I choose, but she's a pseudo-mother figure to Luke, so that makes her this baby's pseudo-grandmother.

"Oh my goodness!" she exclaims quietly so as not to draw Luke's attention. She grabs me into a hug, and then she drags me into the laundry room so we can talk without worrying about him overhearing. The smell of detergent rushes to my nose, and my stomach feels suddenly queasy. "Congratulations! How are you feeling?"

I shrug. "Pretty good. No real symptoms like you hear about."

"And you haven't told him?" she asks.

I shake my head. "Every time I try, another bomb is dropped. I just found out a few days ago myself. I haven't figured out how to tell him."

"Oh, honey," she says. "You need to tell him. This could be exactly what pulls him out of this horrible funk. It'll give him purpose."

I nod as tears pinch behind my eyes. "He was just so relieved that Michelle's baby wasn't his..."

She gives me a stern look. "He was relieved he wasn't going to be tied to that horrible woman for the rest of his life. But it had to come as a blow that he thought he was having a child and then that was taken away from him."

"He just said he was glad, and that's made it even harder to figure out how to tell him." I set a hand on my lower stomach to try to ease the queasiness. I need to get out of this room. I always loved the smell of detergent, but suddenly it's putrid.

"Has he talked to you about his feelings at all?" she asks. "Not about Michelle, but about the loss?"

I shake my head.

"Then you don't really know how he's feeling. I suspect he's numbing more than just his knee with those painkillers."

"But this baby doesn't make up for the loss of that one."

"No," she says, shaking her head, "it doesn't. You're right. But it gives him something new. It gives him a future to look forward to with the woman he loves."

"I'll talk to him," I promise. "And now I need to get out of here. This detergent is making me nauseous."

She laughs. "Oh, I remember those days. Just you wait."

I emerge from the laundry room with hope, and I gulp in breaths of air that's not filled with the perfumed scent of detergent. I march right to the family room because she's right. Luke and I need to talk about his feelings. He needs to unload whatever he's holding inside, and then I can give him our good news, and fingers crossed he'll see it as good news, too.

When I get to him, he's watching football. It's some game he recorded, and he rewinds and studies the same play over and over. At least it's not the one where he got hurt.

Pepper's head rests on his good leg, and he absently strokes her ears with one hand while working the remote with the other.

"Can we talk?" I ask.

"After the game," he grunts.

"After the game you've seen a thousand times?"

He doesn't even acknowledge me.

I wonder if he'd even notice if I moved out...not that I have anywhere to go.

"Have you done your stretches?" I ask.

"No." He rewinds the same play to watch it again.

"So, to be clear, you'd rather watch a game you've already seen than have a conversation with me about something important."

He finally glances over at me. He raises both brows. "Uh, yeah. That about sums it up." His eyes return to the television.

I know this is the knee injury talking. This is his pain talking. This isn't him. This is the exact attitude he warned me about, and Josh warned me about, and even Debbie, to some extent, when she warned me that I need to be the strong woman he fell in love with.

She's right.

And I refuse to take his shit any longer.

I grab the remote out of his hand, and his brows dip in surprise. "Hey!" he exclaims.

I turn off the television and throw the remote out of his reach.

"What the fuck?" he says.

"This has to stop," I yell at him as I fold my arms across my chest.

He stares at me like I've grown two heads. Before he gets a chance to protest, I get a little more passionate.

"I've let your bad attitude slide because you had my sympathy. But I refuse to be your punching bag, and I refuse to sit meekly by while you treat me like garbage. Josh told me not to take your shit, and he's right. So you're going to do your damn stretches and you're going to talk to me while you do them."

He looks surprised. "You can't tell me what to do," he says. I figured he'd put up a fight.

"Uh, yeah, I can. If you can't bear weight on that knee yet, you're pretty dependent on me. And if you can be a dick to me, I can be a bitch back."

He huffs out an annoyed sigh, a signal I've won this battle.

I sit on the edge of the chaise lounge and help brace his foot so he can do his knee exercises. In other words, I'm *forcing* him to do his knee exercises by basically doing them for him. He winces as I lift his leg, but he pulls it up to an angle to stretch it anyway. "You haven't told me how you're feeling about finding out Michelle's baby isn't yours."

"Yeah I did," he says. "Relieved, remember?"

"Right, relieved you won't be tied to Michelle, but what about the actual *baby*?"

"Oh," he murmurs. I watch his eyes carefully. They're focused down on his knee as he holds the stretch we're supposed to hold for a full minute. "I guess I was sort of excited about the idea of it, but I didn't let myself get attached since I never really believed it was mine."

"And how about finding out it's Jack's?" I ask.

"It was Jack's way of getting me back for sleeping with Savannah." His tone is bitter. I don't say anything because I sense he's going to say more, and he does. "When I ended things with her, she told me she was going to fuck my brother.

I told her to go for it, and I told him to go for it, too. She said it to hurt me, thinking in some twisted way I'd grab her back into my arms and defend what we had. But I never felt about her the way she felt about me. I'm just glad she's his problem now."

"What a mess," I say. I help him straighten his leg out. "Do your heel slides now."

He pushes his heel forward and flexes it back as we continue our conversation. "Where's all this coming from?" he asks.

"I just don't want you to hold all that inside." I watch his leg as he keeps flexing his heel. "I want you to know you can unload those things on me and I'm here to help you deal with them."

I glance up at him, and his eyes meet mine. For the first time in days, they soften. "Thank you," he murmurs. "You're a good person, and I'm quite sure I don't deserve you."

I give him a small smile. "You deserve everything, Luke. You've been hit with one thing after another, and we're married. That means we share in both the joy and the sorrow."

"You got any joy in there? Because the sorrow seems to be taking over lately."

My heart races. This is it. The *right* moment to finally tell him. "Um, yeah. Actually, I do have something," I say.

And just as I open my mouth to finally unload this happy secret, the doorbell rings.

CHAPTER 13

I spot a manilla envelope on the porch leaning against the front door when I open it. I glance around, but there aren't any cars or people around, so I have no idea who just rang the bell and left an envelope. I grab it and see a post-it note stuck to the top of it.

Luke—
It's about time this came out.
XO, S

Something feels wrong. My gut tells me who the S is, and if it's Savannah, my gut is also telling me that what's inside has something to do with the secret truths she holds—secrets that could hurt not just Luke's reputation and career, but also his brother's.

More upheaval.

But we need to know what's in that envelope. We need to brace for whatever it is that *S* thinks needs to come out.

I hand Luke the envelope. "This was on the porch," I say as I sit beside him.

He glances at the note stuck to the top, and his eyes move to meet mine. "Oh, shit."

He rips open the envelope, and we both look at the words printed across the top of the page.

For Immediate Release

The headline is printed immediately below that in bold letters: **Fraud, Illegal Substances, and the Dalton Brothers**

And the subtitle paints an even worse picture: *Video Evidence Emerges in Dalton Brothers Scandal*

"Shit," Luke says. He sits up a little and winces. "Is she fucking kidding me? Get my phone. I need my phone."

I jump up and look around for it. "Where is it?" I yell, and he reaches into his pocket.

"I have it," he mutters. "Goddammit." He pulls up a contact, and a few beats later, he starts yelling. "What the fuck do you think you're doing?"

I've never seen him so angry. I can tell he wants to get up and pace around, but he can't. He's a caged tiger, and I don't know what sort of ferocity he's going to unleash.

Just when we had a breakthrough. Just when things were finally looking up. Just when I was about to tell him the truth about our baby.

Impeccable fucking timing, Savannah.

I go immediately into publicist mode despite the fury searing through me.

Damage control.

What can we do to fix this? How can we get ahead of it? Is it already released? Is it coming tomorrow? Or is this simply a threat?

Whatever the case, I need to set my emotions aside. Luke needs me to be calm because he certainly isn't.

"If you send this to the press, that invalidates our contract. No more bonus checks, princess." He listens to whatever lies she spouts for a beat.

"You'll pay for this, Savannah," he hisses, and then he ends the call before he throws his phone across the room. It hits the wall and leaves a dent. "Fuck!" he yells. He grabs his hair with both hands and pulls.

"What did she say?" I ask, trying to keep calm for him. I pick up his phone. It has a nice new crack in the screen.

His fists are clenched and his nostrils flare. His chin is tipped up, revealing an angry vein in his neck. He's fucking *livid* right now, and I have no idea how to calm him down.

He draws in a deep breath.

"I need some whiskey," he says.

"You shouldn't mix—" I begin.

"I know what I should and shouldn't do. I need a fucking glass of whiskey."

Whoa.

I scramble off the couch and pour two fairly tall glasses before I remember *I can't have one.*

I hand him one. I'll take care of the other one later.

He gulps it down and winces. "More."

"Luke," I plead.

He nods to the cup, and I bring him the other one.

Once that one's empty, too, he finally says, "She already sent it to the press because, according to her, she doesn't need my money anymore."

My brows dip. "Why not?"

"Because she's engaged, and she won't get my alimony checks anymore when she remarries. Checks that, by the way, have a little extra in them each month to keep her quiet about this." He holds up the papers, and then he rips them to shreds and tosses them on the floor.

I don't blame him, though I'm certainly annoyed by it since he's not the one who's going to have to clean them up.

"Who the hell would marry her?" I ask.

"A young, dumb kid who believes she can help seal his spot on the Aces," he mutters. He glances up and his eyes meet mine. "Tristan Higgins."

"Tristan Higgins? Isn't he, like, twenty?"

"Twenty-three," he mutters.

"And she's..."

"Robbing the goddamn cradle at thirty-three," he finishes.

Sort of like Luke is, I refrain from pointing out. There's ten years between them. There's six years between us.

"But why would she print this trash?" I ask.

"Because it'll hurt my reputation and solidify Tristan's spot on the team." His tone is pointed, like he doesn't really get how I didn't put that together myself.

"How?" I ask, my brows drawing together in confusion.

"She's been holding onto this shit for eight goddamn years. She was waiting for the right moment, and now that I'm hurt, she can stoke the fears that I'll do the same thing this time. She'll kill my rep, make everyone think I cheated to get healthy, all my sponsors will drop me, and nobody will want me on their team." His tone is full of exhaustion, his speech is starting to slur, and I'm a little scared that he just drank all that whiskey while he's on pain meds. That could be a dangerous combination.

"Why, though? Why would she want to hurt you after all this time?"

"Because I married you. Because I moved on. Because the way she sees it, I'm happy and she's..." He shrugs, but it's half-hearted. He seems worn down. "Her name is fading from the media because she isn't married to a football player anymore. She's crying for attention, and she's hoping this story will get her name back out there. She was just waiting for me to get injured again to blow this shit up."

"Well, good thing you've got a publicist to fix all this," I say. I'm definitely biting off more than I can chew with that statement, but I have to give him hope.

Maybe a baby could give him hope, too? Something to look forward to in the not-so-distant future?

Now's not the time, obviously. And especially not after his next statement.

"Jesus, I can't imagine one more damn thing piled on top of me." He shakes his head. "At least Michelle is out of the picture. But what the fuck is coming next?"

What the fuck is coming next, indeed.

CHAPTER 14

"Hmm, how to get in front of this..." I say aloud, pacing my office. I'm going to wear a path in the purple rug if I don't stop. And then it hits me.

I stop and stare out the window for a few beats as the idea takes root. Luke is going to *hate* it, but hearing from the source himself before the press release hits the news is the only way to get ahead of it.

My phone pings just as I think it.

Too late, I realize as I check the notification. He's already hit one sports news website, and more will surely follow. And that just means we need to set my idea in motion quickly.

I find Luke on the couch watching football in the same place he's been for the last week and a half except for bathroom breaks, sleep, and the occasional meal at the table.

"It already hit one news outlet, so we need to act fast," I say.

"Dammit," he mutters. "I was hoping it was just some sick joke."

"Afraid not, my friend."

"So what's your plan?" he asks.

"I need you to get on camera. Go live in your Instagram stories. Tell your fans that you made a mistake when you were younger, but you won't do the same thing this time. I can draft you a statement to read from or give you talking points, your choice."

He shakes his head. "Abso-fucking-lutely not."

I roll my eyes. "It's a double whammy, Luke. You'll be showing everybody that you're still alive, and you'll be responding to a story that's just starting to hit the press. This way *we* tell the narrative instead of Savannah."

"Let her do her damage," he mutters. "It's all over anyway."

"What's all over?" I ask.

He just glares at me.

Fine. If that's how he wants to play it, then I need to call in the big guns. I think of the person Luke seems to respect most in the world. I need him here.

I head back to my office and make a call.

"Ellie?" the voice on the other end answers.

"I need your help," I say. I explain everything, and an hour later, the doorbell rings. When I open it, I find Coach Thompson and his wife, Mama Mo.

"Please talk some sense into him," I tell Coach, and he nods as I let them in.

"Who was at the door?" Luke yells when he hears the door click shut.

"Me," Coach says.

I spot Luke sit up a little straighter and pause the television as Coach walks into the room. He sits on the edge of the chaise lounge where Luke is propped.

Luke's eyes flick to me, and I swear I see a bit of a glare there...but I don't care. This is for his own damn good.

"What's going on, Luke?" Coach asks.

"You already know or you wouldn't be here."

"Don't you dare give me attitude after I came for a house call," Coach warns.

Luke blows out a breath. "My second year playing, I got hurt. I was young and dumb and took some pills from someone I trusted, the same woman who penned the article hitting the news right now. I didn't know they were a banned substance. I got slapped with a random drug test the day after I learned they were illegal, and my brother switched the sample for me."

"Stupid," Coach says. "On both your parts." He shakes his head. "But you were young. I can understand how you were scared. Your brother, though, should've known better."

"We both know that now, and believe me, this has torn our relationship apart. My relationship with my entire family...it's been eight years, and we're still not past it. We're still not half as close as we used to be."

Mo grabs my hand and squeezes it while Coach whistles through his teeth. "You know the league's going to open an investigation."

He nods. "Yeah, I know."

"Only because it's public," Coach amends. "My guess is you'll both get maybe one game and a fine."

"Jack's going to fucking kill me if he gets suspended."

Coach stands and paces a little in front of Luke. "He's not innocent if he took the test for you."

"No," Luke concedes, "but he did it to protect me."

Coach sighs, and Mo squeezes my hand again as we stand quietly bearing witness to this conversation.

"What's the best course of action here?" Luke asks.

Coach shrugs. "Are you denying it or admitting it?"

"I won't lie," Luke says, and there's the man I fell in love with. The one who's brave and noble and truthful.

"Then get ahead of it. Do what your wife is suggesting. One of the most powerful things you could do is admit you made a mistake in the past and show people how you've learned from it." Coach glances over at me. "It's a smart move. There's a reason she's the publicist."

"Fine," Luke mutters.

Thank you, I mouth to Coach. He nods once and presses his lips together.

"Now where are those granola bars?" he asks.

Luke laughs. "How'd you know I have some?"

Coach's brows draw together. "How do you think Ellie bribed me to come over?"

We all enjoy some of the most delicious homemade peanut butter chocolate chip granola bars I've ever tasted in my life while I go over the talking points I want Luke to hit, and suddenly I understand why Coach has been missing Luke in the locker room. Well, the granola bars plus Luke's sweet, sweet ass...I mean his *talent*.

Yeah, his talent.

I have him practice his statement a few times and I coach him on tone and delivery. Then Coach and Mo help me get Luke into his office, where he takes a seat behind his desk with his leg propped. He wears an Aces t-shirt and a ballcap, still a freaking hot thirst trap if I've ever seen one, and behind him are plaques and trophies and books.

Coach, Mo, and I stand behind my phone so Luke can pretend he's just having a conversation with us. We all nod encouragingly, and then I hit the *live* button for him to start talking.

"Hey everyone." His voice is subdued. "I've never gone live before, but I wanted to come on here today for two reasons. The first is to let you know I'm doing well. Doctors are confident I'll be able to start my physical therapy in the next week, and the swelling is nearly gone. My wife has been forcing me to do my leg exercises to help get me strong and healthy." He glances at me and waves me over. I shake my head, and he says quietly, "Come on."

This was not one of the talking points.

I walk over and smile and wave at the camera, wishing I would've at least had time to fix my hair. I hear my mother's voice in my head. *Put on a little lipstick!*

I get out of the shot as soon as I can.

"That was her, and she's been amazing through all this along with my best friend Josh Nolan and Coach Thompson." He draws in a deep breath. "The second reason I wanted to come on today is to talk about something my ex-wife is publishing in the news. I guess she has some evidence of a mistake I made early in my career, and I just want to address it before it hits the gossip sites. Eight years ago, I took some meds I didn't know were banned. I trusted someone I never should have trusted, and it got me into trouble. I'm sorry for anyone I've disappointed because of this, and most of all, I'm sorry to my family and friends. I'm sorry to those who've kept this secret for many years, and I'm sorry I wasn't truthful about it sooner. I will take whatever punishment the league decides I deserve, and if you feel the need to judge me, do it by my proven performance on the field and the character I've demonstrated over the last eight years." He presses his lips together. "I can't wait to return next season stronger than ever because of the hard work I will put in to get healthy the right, legal way. Thank you."

I end the live chat and click off my phone before any of us talk. He did what he was supposed to do, and he made no mention of Jack. That way, his brother can address the news however he wants.

And now we wait for the proverbial shit to hit the fan.

CHAPTER 15

"Time for your stretches," I call from the kitchen. It's Sunday evening, my night to cook, and this week I went for an easy pork tenderloin with rice and roasted vegetables. I've just finished cutting up the veggies to put them in the oven and I have a couple minutes to help.

I head into the family room, where Luke's on the couch watching football as he has been all day (–slash—all week). The Aces won today, and handily against what Luke proclaimed to be the worst team in the league as he yelled at the television.

"Stretches," I demand, and he huffs out a sigh. I widen my eyes pointedly. I'm not really in any mood to deal with his petulance.

He caves with reluctance as he gets his leg into place for the first exercise. I help him hold it there. All the exercises together take about ten minutes, but you'd think it takes all day based on how hard it is to get him to do them.

It's been a fairly quiet weekend given what Luke confessed to on his Instagram live the other day, and I keep waiting for the phone to ring.

It hasn't.

Or maybe it has and Luke has ignored it. On the other hand...maybe it has and Luke just hasn't told me.

Though the people who'd call have been a little busy with things like, you know, football games. Now that the day games are over and the Sunday night game is set to begin in just forty-five minutes, most of the teams are either home or traveling back, and the league can start looking into this scandal.

At least, according to Luke they can.

And no sooner do I run all that through my thought process than Luke's phone starts to ring.

He checks the screen and mutters a curse. "Hey, Jack," he answers. He puts it on speaker and sets it beside him on the couch as we start the heel slides.

I hold my reaction inside, but anxiety darts through my chest.

"What the fuck have you done?" Jack's voice is accusatory through the phone.

Luke lets out a sigh, and when he speaks, he sounds exhausted. "I got ahead of it and decided to let you handle it your own way."

"You didn't think of letting me know it was hitting the media?" he demands.

"I assumed Savannah took care of that," Luke says.

"Well she didn't. It was the talk of my locker room this morning, and it was enough of a distraction that we lost."

Luke raises his brows and can't hide his smile, which thankfully Jack can't see because I could imagine him punching it right off his little brother's face with how angry he sounds. "Nice. Blame me for your entire team's loss. I'm sure it had nothing to do with the fact that the Chargers are just a better team."

"Oh, fuck you, Luke. You want to hear something even richer?"

"Hit me with it, big man," Luke says. "Can't get much worse over here."

I'm a little more aggressive than I should be when I help him slide his heel down again. I don't mean to be, but I'm really getting tired of him bellyaching about how bad he has it. So he hurt his knee. It'll heal. So his career might be over. He's got a wife who loves him and a baby on the way he still doesn't know about. He still has a future. He still has the entire rest of his life ahead of him, and I'm sick and tired of him acting like his life is over because of an injury.

His brows turn down and he winces.

"Sorry," I mutter.

"My coach has informed me that the league has opened an investigation. Since it's in the media, they're going to make examples out of us," Jack says.

"Goddammit," Luke mutters. "I'm sorry."

"That doesn't change the fact that I might get a suspension because of your stupidity."

"Ream me out all you want, Jack, but you didn't have to take that test for me, and you also didn't have to fuck my ex-girlfriend and knock her up. So save the holier than thou speech. Neither of us is innocent, and we're both going to face whatever consequences the league issues."

"Michelle has nothing to do with this," Jack hisses.

"Oh, doesn't she? You mean you didn't revenge fuck her and accidentally do something you can't take back now? Talk about consequences. Enjoy your life with that nightmare. I'll be going now." Luke cuts the call and tosses his phone against the wall again.

"Goddammit, Luke!" I yell at him. I drop his leg, and he hisses through the pain. "Stop throwing your damn phone!" I pick it up and toss it at him, and then I run into the kitchen to get the hell away from him.

My emotions are big right now, and they're all over the damn place. I'm mad at Luke, and I'm angry with Jack, too, for calling just to put Luke into another funk. I'm tired of everything, but mostly I'm tired of keeping this secret. I'm tired of going through this alone except for a few days a week when the one person I've told does what she can to take a little extra care of me for the few hours she's around.

He's fuming from Jack's call, and while I've already started to learn there's absolutely no ideal time to give him this news, I also know this moment right now certainly isn't even close to a possibility.

Tomorrow.

I'll tell him tomorrow.

Luke's phone rings again, and I hear him answer it. He puts it on speaker again, and it's loud enough that I can hear it from where I stand in the kitchen.

"Hey, Coach."

"I'm calling to let you know the league has opened an official investigation. I'm sorry, Luke."

Luke sighs. "I heard. What's your guess?"

"It happened eight years ago. If it wasn't in the media, they wouldn't even give it a second glance."

"Fucking Savannah," Luke mutters.

"It should be pretty cut and dry. I'd guess you'll know before the end of the week."

"The end of the week is when I'm supposed to start PT," Luke says. "If I'm cleared, anyway."

"Right, and if you get a suspension, you won't have access to our staff. Dr. Charles recommended a few private practices for both doctors and physical therapists, and I've got Mo narrowing it down to the best ones just in case. We'll have your information transferred to them in the event you need to start and can't do it with the team doctors. I'm hopeful it won't come to that."

"Thanks," Luke murmurs. "Can you level with me a second?"

"Of course."

"How bad does this look to Calvin?"

Coach lets out an audible sigh through the phone. My buzzer beeps on my tenderloin, so I take it out to let it rest a few minutes while I strain to hear what he says.

"It doesn't look good, Luke, but I think what you said in that live thing hit where it was supposed to. You were young, and Cal is judging you by your current commitment and performance, the injury notwithstanding."

"That's helpful at least."

My heart soars that my idea actually worked to sort of get Luke back into Calvin's good graces. Between that and the fact that Michelle isn't carrying his kid, there has to be some way to mend their relationship so Calvin isn't searching for ways to get rid of Luke. "Keep me in the loop."

"As long as I can, kid. As long as I can."

"Thanks, Coach." The call ends, and I pull out the vegetables, slice the meat, and make our plates.

"You want to eat in the kitchen or in there?" I yell.

"Kitchen," he yells back.

I help him up, and it's only then I realize I don't know if it's actually okay for me to be helping to lift him. I'm not supposed to lift more than twenty-five pounds according to the literature I read in the *welcome to being pregnant* bag I got from the doctor. I may be bearing more than twenty-five pounds of his weight as he uses me as a crutch to stand.

He hobbles over to the table with his arm around me, and it's good to see him up and moving around. Once we're seated and I've turned off the television, I start up a conversation.

"So what did Coach say?" I ask.

"Like you didn't hear," he says.

I narrow my eyes at him. "Look, I'm trying to be nice and make conversation. You can either choose to participate in that with me or you can be rude."

His brows dip. "What's gotten into you lately?"

A baby is the answer to that question. A baby is *literally* what has gotten into me.

"Oh, did you want me to go back to being your punching bag? Because I'm tired of it. Everyone keeps telling me not to take any shit from you, so I'm done. You want to act like a child? Go for it. I'll treat you like one."

His brows lift a little. It almost seems like he *likes* when I'm mean to him.

Well buckle up, babe. My emotions are hot right now.

I've got a whole lot more where that came from.

CHAPTER 16

When I said yesterday that I'd tell him tomorrow, I had no idea that *tomorrow* would bring the league's decision about his punishment. It's when I'm done with my morning shower, dressed and ready for another day of taking care of Luke in between work, when I learn what just happened.

I hear Luke yelling, and I rush down to see what's going on.

I spent the entire shower rehearsing how I'd say the words. I even mouthed them to myself as I put on my make-up and dried my hair.

I was so ready to tell him, so hopeful after a nice breakfast where I felt like things were moving in the right direction for us...but the yelling tells me I won't get to.

He throws his phone *again* just as I walk into the room.

I don't bother picking it up, but there's another dent in the wall and probably another crack in the screen.

His arms are folded across his chest as he fumes, and he glares at me and then at his phone. "Well, I can't get up and punch a hole in the wall, so that's how I'm taking out my aggression. Move on or deal with it."

"What the hell happened from breakfast to now?" I demand.

"Coach just called to let me know I'm suspended for two games and I have to pay fifty grand," he spits. "Jack got one game and the same fine."

My brows dip. I'm a little slow here. "I know this isn't the news you wanted, but is it that big a deal when you can't play anyway? Isn't it better to be suspended now than when you're playing?"

He blows out a frustrated breath. "I still get paid on the injury report. I don't get paid when I'm suspended."

"So fifty grand plus..." I trail off and wait for him to fill in the blank.

"A little over a hundred and sixty K for two games."

My eyes widen. I had no idea what his salary was...and I guess I still don't. So a mistake he made eight years ago is going to cost him over two hundred grand. Those numbers are unfathomable to me.

"And worse, I can't have any contact with the entire Aces organization, which means I can't go there for my exam or to start my PT later this week."

"I heard Coach say something about that to you. He's setting you up with a private practice, right? This won't delay your recovery, Luke."

He purses his lips. "He can set me up wherever he wants. I'm not going."

"Stop it," I say like I'm dealing with a child. "Yes, you are."

"No, I'm not. I want to work with Dr. Charles. I want Adrian, the team trainer, taking me through my therapy. Not some stranger."

"It doesn't matter who it is," I say.

He looks at me like I'm dumb. "I trust those people. I don't trust some random therapist I've never even met before."

I sigh as I'm faced with yet another obstacle from a very stubborn man.

His phone rings again. "That'll be Jack." He nods to his phone. "Can you hand it over?"

All Jack is going to do is shake Luke's anger even more. I spot the incoming call: *Jack Dalton.*

I raise a brow and shake my head before I walk past his phone and breeze out of the room. "I told you to stop throwing it. And do your damn exercises. I have work to do."

I hear him mutter something under his breath. Oh, did I make him mad? Well good. He needs to step up and start acting like a man.

But over the course of the next couple days, that's the last thing he does.

He refuses to do his exercises.

His agent calls. One of his sponsors dropped him, just another event in a long succession of things that digs in to hurt a little more.

He wallows. This isn't fun or enjoyable, but it's what I signed up for. I love him despite his poor attitude, and maybe it's my job to help bring him back to himself.

On Thursday morning, I catch him attempting to *walk.*

"What the hell are you doing?" I yell at him.

"I'm fine," he mutters.

"You are not fine. You just had major surgery and your doctor told you not to bear any weight until your next check. And even when you are allowed to put weight on it, you'll need to wear a brace."

"What difference does it make? Between my age, my injury, and my reputation, nobody's going to want Luke Dalton playing for them. It's too expensive and too risky."

I don't know what to say to that, but I do help him back to the couch, where he can continue sitting and wallowing.

Mo calls me with the information for the doctor Luke is scheduled to see on Friday.

He refuses to go.

I call Mo back on Thursday evening when I'm sure he won't leave the house.

"Then I'll get this doctor to make a house call," she says.

"Won't that be expensive?" I ask.

"Ask your hubby."

On Friday morning a little before his appointment, I find Luke stretched out on the couch. His knee is no longer elevated, and when I ask him why, he tells me it's because it doesn't hurt anymore. When the doorbell rings, he looks at me with narrowed eyes. I just shrug innocently and greet our visitor at the door.

"Dr. Shepard?" I ask the mid-forties man standing there, and he nods. "Come on in. Luke doesn't know you're coming, so we're all in for a nice surprise."

The doctor laughs and follows me into the family room. "I have a visitor for you," I say brightly.

Luke doesn't move, but he does pause the game he's watching.

"I'm Dr. Shepard. Monique sent me over since you refused to come in person. Can I take a look at your knee?"

Luke sighs, and I think for a second he might tell the doctor no...but eventually he relents after letting us all know that *this is bullshit.*

The doctor examines his knee. "Stand up for me and walk," he says after a while, and Luke does. "And sit." Once he does, the doctor gives him the assessment. "You're healing well. I'm officially clearing you to start your physical therapy. Any time you're up and moving around, you need to wear this brace." He pulls a brace as if by magic out of his bag. "But you can start slowly regaining strength. Take it easy, and listen to your physical therapist. If you want to get better in time for next season, I suggest you keep doing your exercises and attend your doctor's appointments."

"Yes, sir," Luke says sullenly. I thought he'd be a little more excited about being cleared to start physical therapy, but I guess this is where the real work begins.

He can't just wallow on the couch anymore with the doctor's permission. Now he needs to work to regain the strength and movement he had before the injury.

But at least maybe he'll get his ass off the couch—and maybe, for the love of God, we can watch something other than football once in a while.

CHAPTER 17

The physical therapist visits us later in the afternoon, and he gives Luke a whole new list of exercises to do. He calls it Luke's *homework*, and it includes stairs one at a time with the sage advice of *up with the good knee, down with the bad.*

Luke is *thrilled* to leave the guest room behind to sleep in the master bedroom again, and I waste no time in moving our comforter and phone chargers back upstairs once he's done his first round of homework by climbing the steps.

I find him standing in the closet with a folder in his hands when I'm done plugging in his charger.

"What's this?" he asks softly.

My eyes widen as they zero in on what he's holding.

Welcome to Motherhood!

The letters are big and bold on the outside of the folder.

"I, uh..." I say, all the blood draining from my face. "I can explain."

And here's the explanation: I didn't feel the need to hide the bag since nobody was actually entering this closet except me.

He nods as if to encourage me to explain, and he's back to hiding his emotions. I have no idea what he's thinking. None. I can't tell if he's tired or sad or wary or happy or indifferent.

"Um..."

"Are you...?" he trails off.

I swallow as I try to get past the sudden lump in my throat.

I don't know how he's going to take this, but I haven't known all along—which is why I still haven't said anything. Our emotions are frayed. He's in a fragile state right now.

But it's time for the truth to come out.

My chest races with anxiety as I whisper, "Yes." I'm terrified as I say the single syllable that will mean an entirely new world to us both.

Will I have to do this alone?

Will he be part of this with me?

Will this be the thing that pushes him over the tipping point? Or will it miraculously be the thing that not only brings us closer together but makes him see that his future is rife with possibilities?

His eyes dip down to the folder before they move back to me. "How far along?"

"Almost nine weeks," I say, tears heating behind my eyes.

"Nine—" he stops himself short as if he's counting backwards. "That's right before training camp started."

I nod.

"So you're due..."

"April nineteenth." I tip up my chin nervously.

"It's mine?" he asks cautiously.

I should be insulted by the question, and if it were anybody else, I might be. But I know this man has had at least three women claim that they were pregnant with his child when they weren't. "I've only been with you since the day I met you," I murmur. "Nearly twenty-four hours a day, too."

He doesn't react with a chuckle like I'd expect.

"And I'll take a paternity test to prove it. I have nothing to hide, Luke. It's yours, no question and no doubt."

He blows out a long breath, and it almost feels like he's biding time because he doesn't quite know how to react. His eyes move all around the closet before they land back on me.

"I just..." he begins. "I need a minute."

I nod, but his words kill a huge part of me. I wanted him to react with excitement. Nerves, sure, and maybe a little bit of fear—those are natural, of course—but I wanted the dominating feeling to be one of happiness.

That doesn't appear to be what I'm getting.

"I'll leave you alone," I say, and I walk out of the closet as tears pinch behind my eyes.

I head downstairs and fall onto the couch, where I cry for this baby and for myself and for how freaking *alone* I feel in this moment.

I cry for him finding out in a way I wasn't expecting. I wanted to be the one to tell him, to find some special way, and now I won't get that.

And he needs a minute.

I don't even know what that means. It could mean one minute, or it could mean forever. The one comfort I have to hold onto right now is that he didn't kick Michelle out until he had evidence the baby wasn't his. I'd imagine he'd at least extend the same shelter courtesy to the mother of his *actual* child, especially given that I'm his best friend's little sister.

But maybe this is all just too much for him. He's already overwhelmed, and he's exhausted, and he's been so down about the future. I was hopeful that this would be the good news to pull him out of that, but with his completely blank expression, I have no idea where his head is at.

It's more than a minute when I hear his voice at the top of the stairs. "Ellie?"

I move over toward the stairs and find him slowly descending them. Good leg first, bad leg second, one at a time, and pausing between steps like just taking a stair is taxing for him. It probably is. He's basically laid on the couch for the last two weeks, so this is a lot of movement.

"Do you need help?" I ask.

He nods, and I move toward the landing and help him move slowly down from there to the bottom. We move toward the kitchen, and he leans on the counter.

He studies me for a beat before he asks a question. "How did this happen? I thought you were on the pill."

My heart drops.

That is his first response? *I thought you were on the pill?*

I don't think he wants this baby, and I don't think he wants me, either.

A pang of devastation stabs my chest.

"I *was* on the pill," I confirm, my voice shaking with emotion. "And I stopped taking it when I found out. The doctor said there are a lot of things that could make it ineffective. My best guess is either alcohol or allergy medication."

"I'm sorry," he says.

"For what?" I ask, glancing up at the ceiling as I try my hardest to ward off the tears I feel pinching behind my eyes.

"I should've known." His words incite the first glimmer of hope I've felt since he found the folder in the closet. It's so *him* to be hard on himself over something that was completely out of his control. "I should've seen the signs. I shouldn't have been so wrapped up in my own misery that I couldn't tell something was going on with you."

"You couldn't have known."

"It's all so obvious now." He sighs softly. "That's why you asked how I felt about the *baby*, not about *Michelle*." He says the words as if a sudden lightbulb goes off, like he's connecting the dots of the last few weeks.

I nod.

"And *supporting me* by not drinking? I should've known then."

I can't help a tiny smile. "Don't be too hard on yourself. I've been pretty good about keeping it quiet."

He presses his lips together. "How long have you known?"

I clear my throat. "Officially? About a week."

"But you've suspected since..." he trails off and waits for me to fill in the blank.

"Since the night you got hurt," I admit. "I realized I was late as I was scrolling my calendar."

His eyes widen. "That's almost three weeks. You've been going through this for three weeks by yourself?"

I nod.

"Does anybody know?"

"Debbie," I admit.

"Debbie?" he repeats, clearly shocked that she's the one person I've told.

"It just sort of came out one day," I murmur.

He narrows his eyes. "When were you going to tell me?"

I lift a shoulder as a tear splashes over my lid and onto my cheek. "I went to the doctor the day before Savannah released her article. I wanted to tell you a million times, but it was one thing after another. First the article. Then Jack being an asshole. Then the suspension. I didn't know how to pile one more thing on top of all that, especially not when you were so grateful Michelle's baby wasn't yours."

"I was grateful I didn't have to deal with Michelle," he notes quietly. "I'm sorry I made you feel like you couldn't tell me, but the paternity test results were devastating. It was the third time I felt like a baby was taken away from me because of someone else's lie."

"And now?" I ask, settling a hand on the belly that's only a couple weeks away from growing more and more until I deliver the sweet baby developing inside.

"This feels different than the other three," he says softly, and his words send a pulse of relief through my spine. "This feels like mine."

He shifts to move in a little closer to me, and he rests his hand over mine where it lies on my stomach. He leans down to press a kiss to my lips, the first real sign of affection in days. And then he wraps his arms around me and pulls me into him. I rest my head on his chest as the world seems to spin a little differently now.

He still has a long road ahead of him. We still have to deal with ex-wives and ex-girlfriends and people who should support Luke but don't. We still have to deal with the fallout of his suspension and fine, and the hit to his reputation, and whether his career is really over or if he'll get the chance to continue playing.

But together we've created something, a bond that will come to life in seven short months, and we will hold hands and hold each other as we face all those obstacles together.

At least that's my hope in this moment as I finally blow out the breath it seems I've been holding since I first noticed I was late. I hold onto the moment as long as I can before he shifts a little and hisses.

"You need to sit," I say, and he nods.

"So do you," he teases, and it's a tiny glimpse of my Luke, the one who has been missing in action for the last few weeks. My Prince.

I help him over to the couch, where I prop his knee on the same pillows I've propped them on for weeks now. "I need to show you something," I say once I get him into place. I head to my office and fish through my purse, and then I head back toward the couch.

I sit beside him and hand him the picture from my first ultrasound.

"This is it?" he asks, and I nod.

"That little jellybean thing right there is our baby," I say, pointing to it.

"Holy shit," he murmurs as he stares at the little black and white photo. He glances over at me. "How have you been feeling?"

I shrug. "Fine. I honestly don't know that I would've even suspected anything if I hadn't realized the timing."

"I'm sorry I've been so selfish. That changes now."

"You *should* be focused on yourself. You just had major surgery, Luke. It's okay to be selfish. You need to recover and I'm here to take care of you."

"I should've been here to take care of you, too," he says. He pulls on my shoulder so I lean back, and he kisses the top of my head. "And I will be. From now on."

"I'm holding you to that," I say, and I settle back on his chest so we can both stare at our little jellybean.

CHAPTER 18

As I navigate the car onto our street after Luke's second week of physical therapy, a sense of gratitude washes over me.

I guess the folder was meant to be left out in the closet, or I might still be holding onto my secret. Instead, Luke seems to have found the wake-up call he needed. He's been focused on getting himself back together. I found him lifting weights the other day, and he's dedicated to his therapy sessions. We have one more week of intense therapy, and then we start the in-home phase of his healing.

We're getting there. It's an uphill climb, but today's not just the last day of his suspension—it's also the last day of therapy outside of the Aces' facility.

Josh and Nicki are waiting on our front porch when we pull in. We still haven't told anybody about the baby, mostly because technically Luke and Josh weren't supposed to have any contact with each other during the term of Luke's suspension. That hasn't kept *me* away from them, but we want to tell them about the baby together.

The rules are lifted now that he has served his time, and I've been sort of a messenger between my brother and my husband over the last two weeks.

And now we can tell our best friends that we'll have babies just two months apart. I can finally ask my best friend for advice about what the hell to eat since apparently right around week ten was my threshold for feeling good.

I'm exhausted all the time. I haven't gotten sick, but the nausea has been horrid. Mostly I've spent time lying on the couch beside Luke when I'm not driving him to his PT appointments.

If only I felt a little better, maybe we could hit the sheets together. *That* still hasn't happened since before his injury.

"Come on in," I say to Josh and Nicki, and I unlock the door.

"I brought green chili enchiladas!" Nicki says, and she tears the foil off the top of her pan once we're in the kitchen. I want to gag at the smell of the sauce.

"Thank you," I say. I try to inject some enthusiasm, but it's definitely not there.

"What's wrong?" she asks me. "You look a little green."

Luke's eyes widen as he looks at the tray of food and back at me.

"Can we tell them now?" I whisper to Luke.

He chuckles and nods.

"I'm pregnant," I blurt, and the entire room goes quiet for a few beats. "And I haven't been able to eat anything green for the last week," I add into the silence.

And then there's the eruption.

"Oh my God!" Nicki shrieks. She runs over to me and squeezes me.

"Is she serious?" I hear Josh say to Luke over Nicki's squeals.

I giggle at the commotion and the excitement and the *love* in this room.

This is just everything I ever wanted out of life, all coming together in this one room.

"When are you due?" Nicki asks.

"April nineteenth."

"Oh my God, our babies are going to be cousins *and* best friends!" She's giddy with excitement.

"Way to knock up my sister, man," Josh says to Luke, punching him in the arm.

Excited chatter falls over the four of us as Nicki and I talk about everything from morning sickness to baby room themes and I listen to the boys as they discuss financial security and Josh chips in his two cents on the best car seats on the market.

This is family, and when I was dumped and fired on the same day back in Chicago just a few months ago, I never could've imagined this would be my future. When I bumped into a hot guy at the bar and ended up taking him back to my hotel room, I never could've imagined that a few months later, I'd be married to him and having his baby.

I've always been a one door closes and another one opens kind of girl, but I never would've guessed all the doors that would open simply by moving from Chicago to Vegas.

Life moves incredibly fast.

Maybe it took Luke's injury to slow us down a little, and if there's one silver lining to look for, one door opening, it's that.

As I look at the laughter in this room, I'm just glad I've slowed down enough to enjoy the ride.

* * *

When I told Luke about the genetic testing, he didn't want to get it done.

"Will the answers on that test change anything?" he'd asked me, and when I really thought about it, I knew he was right. No. Whatever those tests say, we will love this baby with everything we have.

But when I told him the test also tells us gender a full two months earlier than without the test, he was all in.

113

And so he goes with me to my next doctor's appointment. He wears his knee brace under his jeans and a ballcap pulled down low, and we head into the exam room when the tech calls us back. She takes my weight and blood pressure, and the doctor comes in a few minutes later.

"Want to hear the heartbeat?" she asks.

"Of course," I say.

She squirts the same jelly they use for the ultrasounds on my stomach, and Luke sits in the chair beside me. He reaches for my hand as the doctor moves her wand around, and nerves flit through me at the silence.

Why is it so quiet?

She moves the wand a little to the left.

Is everything okay?

She clears her throat.

I glance over at Luke, whose eyes are glued to the wand, and I'm just about to voice the questions in my mind when the sweet little *whoosh-whoosh-whoosh* calms every fear.

I let out a breath. "There's baby," she says softly. We listen for a few beats. "Baby's heartbeat is one-forty-seven. Perfectly normal."

I let out a breath of relief, and Luke does, too.

We head back to the lab for my blood draw that'll get sent out for the genetic testing, and that's it. We head home after the lab techs let us know we'll have results within a week.

Within a week we'll know if it's a boy or a girl. Blue or pink. Dinosaurs or Minnie Mouse. Football player or cheerleader.

It doesn't matter. I'm excited for either, and if our little boy loves Minnie Mouse or our little girl wants to play football, I'll do everything I can to give them what they want in this life.

And I can't wait for all of it.

Five long days later, I get an email with the lab results.

"Luke!" I yell from my office. He appears in the doorway a minute later.

"Yes, dear?" he asks, and I giggle at his response.

"I got the results," I say.

He grins. "Have you looked yet?"

I shake my head. "I waited for you."

He walks around the desk and stands behind me, and I stand, too.

"What are you thinking?" he asks.

"Boy. I've felt boy since the minute I peed on a stick."

He wrinkles his nose. "Thanks for that visual."

I giggle and lace my arms around his waist. "What are you thinking?"

"Boy." He presses a kiss to my lips.

I pull back and smile. "Ready for this?"

He nods, and I move the desk chair out of the way. I navigate the mouse to the results.

"Do you have a preference one way or the other?" I ask before I click it.

"Healthy. That's all. I feel like with a boy, I'll have a little adventure buddy. With a girl, I'll be your typical protective father. Either way, I'll be thrilled."

"I feel the same way," I say. "Do you have any names you like?"

"Just click the button," he says with a touch of exasperation, and I laugh as I press it.

The very top of the page says *Low Risk* in large letters, and I breathe out a sigh of relief. I hadn't realized how nervous I was that there could be problems until I felt that rush of relief.

And immediately next to *Low Risk*, the *Fetal Sex* is listed as *male*.

We both seem to spot the news at the same time. "Boy!" we both exclaim in unison.

Tears fill my eyes as I realize for the first time that we're having a healthy little baby boy.

We both straighten as we embrace each other and the fact that this is getting more and more real with each passing day. We're getting closer to meeting this little boy, and the closer we get, the more excited I feel about it.

And the more in love I fall with his daddy.

He cups my neck as his eyes find mine. "Congratulations," he says softly.

"Same to you. So, you got any names picked out yet?" I'm teasing, but the mood shifts dramatically from the excitement of what we just found out to something much, much hotter.

He chuckles. "Not yet. You?"

"Maybe one or two," I admit.

"I love you so much, Ellie," he murmurs. His lips brush mine, and after several long weeks apart, I'm finally getting the sense that we're both in a place where we're ready to show each other that love through physical actions.

"Take me upstairs," I say against his lips.

"I was planning to just fuck you right here in your office."

"That'll work, too," I say.

He opens his mouth to mine, and just kissing him brings every feeling I have for him right to the surface. A hot need aches through my entire body. I'm ready for this. For him.

He pulls me more tightly against him, our bodies flush together, and my desire for this man is off the charts. He pushes his hips to mine, and all the stresses and worries of the day melt away here in his arms.

Except one.

How will we actually do this so I don't hurt his knee?

As if he's reading my mind, he leads me over to the couch. He sits, and he indicates that I should lower down on his lap as if he's testing whether that'll work.

"This won't hurt the baby, right?" I ask as I throw one leg on either side of him to straddle him. I shift my hips over him as I get into place, and he moans.

I know the answer to that question I saw in the booklet from the doctor's office and the internet, but I'm still seeking some confirmation from Luke. I'm not sure why. Maybe because he seems to know everything. Maybe because I trust him with my life.

"It won't hurt the baby," he murmurs, and he reaches for the back of my neck as he pulls my mouth down to his.

We kiss there a while, and then he pulls back. "Get naked," he says, and I laugh.

"What a line," I say, but I still get up off his lap and do as I'm told.

He lowers his pants while I remove mine, and then I get back on. I slide down as he holds himself up for me, and we both groan at his entrance. I move over him, up and down, and he holds onto my hips as we find the rhythm that's been missing from our lives for too many weeks.

The connection between us is intense and passionate, and my chest tightens with love as he moves in and out of me. It's pleasure on top of love, and when his eyes meet mine just before he starts to come, I see all the same emotions reflected back at me. It's not just desire and lust, but it's this commitment to each other that formed out of something else entirely.

We're both in this forever, and as he starts to come, he thumbs my clit and pushes me into my own climax. I yell my way through the pleasure as I fight the contractions of my body, and when I come out on the other side, I'm sated and exhausted.

He lets out a long, satisfied sigh when it's over, both of us panting as we try to regain our breath after that powerful ride.

He slips out of me, but neither of us moves for a few beats. He just holds me in his arms there on the couch, and I never want this moment to end.

I finally have my Luke back, and I just hope he stays this time.

CHAPTER 19

It's strange sitting in the same suite with the same women but without the fear stabbing my stomach.

My worst fears were realized when Luke got hurt, but he'll heal. He'll live. It could've been worse, and I'm thankful it wasn't.

My parents are in the suite this time, too, and we all cheer as the Aces' kicker kicks off the first quarter against the Cardinals. Instead of watching the game, I watch my husband on the sidelines. He sits on the bench beside the wide receivers, and he points out things on a tablet. He's not a coach, exactly, but he's helping out where he can.

"Would he want to coach in the future?" my dad asks, nodding toward the field, and I shrug.

"He told me it's bad luck to talk about what comes next, so he hasn't really mentioned it." It's so weird to carry on a conversation with my dad like everything is totally normal. I haven't told them about the baby yet. I'm planning to do it tonight at dinner, but it's all I can think about.

"Ugh!" Nadine snorts behind us. "My husband says that, too. They all have the same superstition, and it drives me crazy. I'd love *some* insight into what my future might look like."

"Right?" I laugh. Part of me wants him to keep playing just because of this club of women I've found, but even if he does, this little club isn't guaranteed. Any number of these players could be traded or cut, and new members could make their way in. The dynamic here will change constantly, and I'm not sure whether that's something I'm cut out for.

I'm just thankful for a friend like Nicki, someone I know will stick around long after the lights turn off on the field.

"Seems to me he'd make a good coach," my dad says.

"I think he would, too," I admit. *By the way, I'm pregnant.*

"Will he keep playing?"

"I don't know," I murmur. *But he did knock me up.* "Depends on his therapy. He's doing great, but he has a long road ahead of him."

Josh catches a ball halfway down the field, and everyone goes wild. I'm thankful for the distraction because I don't know how much longer I can sit here carrying on a conversation without telling my parents about the baby.

The game is long, and I eat a lot of popcorn, but eventually it ends with a victory and we head toward the tunnel and find our players. They're still in the locker room when I spot Savannah.

I assume she's waiting for Tristan, and my blood boils. She doesn't deserve to be back here, not after the way she betrayed Luke.

She has a lot of nerve showing her face here, and I feel a sudden fierce protectiveness wash over me. Maybe it's for the baby and maybe it's for my husband, but something propels my feet in her direction.

I set my hand on my hip as I try to be intimidating, which I'm really not at all, and she blinks over at me like I'm an annoying fly buzzing around.

"Can I help you?" she asks.

"Why would you do that to him?" I demand.

She lifts a shoulder. "He had it coming."

I glare at her. "How? Because he divorced you? Smartest thing he's done aside from marrying me."

She grunts with derision. "Oh, honey, you just go right on believing what you want to believe. He'll treat you like a princess for a few months and then he'll drop you like he always does. Mark my words."

"Like he did to you? Ever think it's because he couldn't stand being with you? That he only stayed as long as he did because he didn't want you blabbing what you knew to the media?"

She narrows her eyes. "Is that what he told you?" She lowers her voice. "I suppose he left out the parts about the wild sex we used to have all over that kitchen counter." She winks at me and lowers her voice to a whisper. "Ask him about *that*. I don't miss being a Dalton, but I do miss that gorgeous cock of his." She tilts her head and gets a faraway, dreamy look in her eye. "His brother's too."

I clench my jaw at her words, and I'm about to issue a very loud, very angry *fuck you* even though my parents are a mere twenty feet away in their own conversation with Nicki when the locker room door opens. I spot Luke, and the words die in my throat as a wave of emotion for this man pours over me.

And *that* is what matters. *We* matter.

Savannah is insignificant. She can try her hardest to tear us apart, to take down Luke, to try to prove he isn't my prince...but she will fail.

Every time.

His eyes scan the room as if he's looking for something, and as soon as they land on me, they soften. He spots who I'm talking to and beelines in my direction.

"So nice of you to chat with the media," Luke says to me. "But we save our comments for respectable news sources, not this trash." He grabs my arm and guides me away from her as she calls out some insult behind us, but I miss it. It doesn't really matter what she says, anyway. What Luke and I have can't be broken by a jealous ex.

"Are you okay?" he whispers in my ear.

"Fine," I mutter.

"She can be a lot to handle." He presses a kiss to my temple.

"She can do her worst, but she won't take us down," I say. I turn my head and catch his lips with mine for a quick, soft kiss that means everything.

Josh is hugging my parents, who congratulate him on an amazing game, and then we all head out. We meet back up at Josh's place—all six of us—for dinner. Nicki has prepared an amazing feast with no green food with the exception of salad, and I stifle a giggle as she winks in my direction while she sets out a bland chicken noodle casserole. She sets a spicy pork dish beside it. I opt for the bland chicken with some focaccia bread, as does she.

"So when are you moving out here?" Josh asks my parents as we all settle into our food.

"We actually looked at a few houses a couple weeks ago when we were out," my mom says. She glances at my dad.

"And our offer was accepted on one about two miles from here," my dad finishes.

"Congratulations!" Josh says, and my eyes widen.

My first thought is that, well, having my parents in Chicago hasn't been half bad as I've been running around having one-night stands and getting knocked up. But my second thought is that it will be freaking amazing to have them nearby as I go through pregnancy and have a baby. There's nothing more important to me than family, and those are values I want to instill in this baby boy—especially given Luke's damaged relationship with his own family.

As much as I don't care for them or the way they treat him, one of my greatest hopes is that someday we can mend those fences. I'm not sure even how that would work, especially since Luke hasn't expressed that as something he wants, but I can't imagine a world where my baby grows up not knowing both sides of his family. I won't push it, though. I've met the Daltons, and I'll understand and respect if Luke has wishes different from my own.

We all express sentiments similar to Josh, and then I ask, "So when do you close?"

My parents glance at each other. "We did. Yesterday."

"What?" I gasp.

"We're just so excited to be here every step of the way as our first grandchild is on its way," my mom looks lovingly at Josh. She turns to me. "And, you know, eventually maybe you'll have kids, too."

I roll my eyes, but then I blurt, "Eventually? Or like two months after Josh and Nicki?"

Her eyes widen and my dad coughs.

"What?" she gasps, mirroring my reaction a few seconds ago.

I laugh and set a hand on my stomach. "I'm pregnant with your second grandchild."

My mom leaps out of her chair to give me a hug, and my dad follows after as my mom embraces Luke. "Oh, honey, I'm so happy," she says as she sits back down.

"And we already know the gender," I add.

"We do too," Josh admits.

"I thought you weren't finding out!" I say.

He shrugs. "We weren't, and then the doctor asked if we wanted to know, and we did."

I laugh. "Well?"

"Let's say at the same time," he suggests.

Luke nods. "One, two, three!"

"Boy!" Josh and I both say at the same time, and my mom starts crying.

Two new baby boys are joining the Nolan clan in just a few months. My mother who has pressed me for grandchildren for at least the last four years is in freaking heaven.

If only this blissful feeling could last.

But I guess it wasn't meant to.

Luke's phone starts ringing just after we walk in the front door from our visit across the street. The smile he's worn most of the night fades as he sees who's calling.

"I already said I'd pay your fine," he answers, and his words paired with his feisty tone tell me it's Jack on the other end of the line. He goes silent, and then all the color drains from his face. "Oh."

I try to wait patiently. Of all the times he *doesn't* have his phone blasting on speaker, it's this one.

"Uh, thanks for letting me know," he says. "I'll be there."

When he hangs up, he stares into space for a few beats, and then he turns to me. "Want to take a trip to Michigan with me?"

My brows dip. "What? Why?"

"My father died."

CHAPTER 20

"What?" I gasp.

"Apparently he had a brain aneurysm." He says it without emotion, but regardless of how close their relationship was, he has to be feeling *some* sort of way about this.

"Oh my God, Luke," I murmur. What do I do? How do I be what he needs in this moment? Those are my first thoughts. I have no idea what this is going to do to him. I'm worried the weight of even more on top of him is going to crush him. But he's strong, and he's got me to hold his hand as we navigate this news. "I'm so sorry."

He ignores my condolence and instead repeats what Jack must've just told him as he stares down at the blank phone in his hand. "Kaylee is with my mom. Jack is flying out tonight. They're planning the arrangements tomorrow." He draws in a breath.

"Are you okay?" I ask. My first instinct is to go into planner mode, to grab us a flight and to get packing, but something tells me he has more to say.

He leans back against the counter and his eyes finally lift to mine. His are filled with shock.

He shakes his head. "No," he says softly. "I'm not."

"Talk to me," I say, matching his tone.

"I just..." he trails off and shrugs. "I figured we had more time. I thought someday we'd fix things. I thought I'd get a chance to apologize and he'd apologize back and we'd put the past behind us. I never thought he'd just..." He stops as if he can't make himself say the words, but then he finishes, "Be gone."

I grab his hands in mine. I have no idea what to say. I've never dealt with losing a parent, and even though my relationship with my parents isn't always perfect, it's still good. It's definitely not broken. And now Luke has to live with that for the rest of his life.

"You can't fix what happened with him," I say, "but maybe that's the lesson. Life is short and precious, and you still have time with your mom and your sister and your brother. If you've ever thought about fixing things, now might just be the time."

His eyes seem to mist over, and he closes them as he bows his head for a beat in what seems like a silent prayer. When he opens his eyes again, they're red.

I step into him and wrap my arms around him. He pulls me closer, clinging to me, and it doesn't matter if they were close or not...this hurts him, which means it hurts me, too.

"I'll get us a flight," I murmur into his chest.

"Thank you," he whispers, and I pull away to get to work.

I book us on the nonstop redeye since it seems like he'll want to get there as soon as possible, and then I run upstairs to pack. I toss in his suit and a demure black dress for myself along with the essentials that'll get us by for a few days.

"Do you want me to book us a hotel?" I ask once I've finished packing.

He shakes his head. "We'll stay at my parents' house." He pauses a beat, then amends his statement to, "My *mom's* house."

I push away how weird that might be for us when his family made it so clear they didn't want us together. I look up whether it's safe for pregnant women to travel, and I find the answer is yes.

We head toward the airport and we're boarding a plane a few hours later. I texted my family to let them know what happened, and Josh made sure to request I send him the information on the arrangements as soon as I have it. I promised I would. I know he has a game to play out of town this Sunday, but I'm sure Luke would appreciate the support of the people he's closest to as we say goodbye to his father.

We land in Detroit a little after three in the morning, which is a little after midnight at home. I'm exhausted, but, then, I'm *always* exhausted lately. I guess it comes with the whole pregnancy territory thing. I'm nauseous, too—something else that's pretty standard these days.

We rent a car and he drives us the half hour to his mom's place, a sprawling mansion in the Detroit suburb of Birmingham. He has a key to the house, and he lets us in. He must've called her to let her know we were on our way since she left a light on, but the house is mostly dark and quiet as we move quietly through it toward the stairs. Together we haul the suitcases up since neither of us can really do it alone, and then he leads me toward a bedroom.

He flips on the light, and I never really thought about what sort of room a young Luke might've grown up in. I wonder how long his parents have lived here, and when he last lived here, and even when he last stayed here.

The furniture is dark wood and the bedding is navy blue. The walls are painted a light blue and are covered in framed jerseys. All Dalton, all number eighty-four, but in several different colors that probably represent high school, college, and eventually the Aces.

If they weren't proud of him...those Aces jerseys would never have made it to the wall. I refrain from pointing that out.

Instead, I wander over to his dresser, where trophies litter the entire dark wood surface. They seem to go on double in the reflection of the mirror. Each trophy has a different figure at the top, but one thing is the same on all of them: every single mini person holds a football. There are a few medals set on top of the dresser, too, and there's no dust, which tells me that even if he hasn't been in here for years, *someone* has.

The medals appear to be from marathons. I didn't even know he was a runner.

I glance at him in the mirror, and I watch as he walks over to the entertainment center. He picks up one of the two photographs set on top and stares at it, and I'm curious enough to walk over to look with him.

I spot a young Luke, maybe early-teens, and a mid-teen Jack. In the middle is Tim, his arm around each of his son's shoulders as Luke holds up a huge fish with a grin. They seem to be on a boat, and they look like the Three Musketeers.

"Did you catch that?" I ask.

Luke nods. "My dad was so proud of me." His voice breaks a little at the end. "It was the summer before my brother started high school. I remember feeling like everything was about to change." He sets the photo down and walks over to the queen bed. He sits on the edge of it. "And it did. That's the last time I can remember feeling like my father was proud of me. All his attention landed on my brother when he nabbed the starting quarterback position as a freshman. Between his own coaching position and my brother, he didn't bother with me. In fact, he basically pawned me off on one of my high school coaches." He shakes his head a little. "I guess I never realized my resentment went back that far."

"Sometimes it takes tragedy for us to weed through our feelings," I muse as I sit beside him.

He glances at me like I just said something very wise, and then he leans over and rests his head on my shoulder. "It doesn't feel real."

"That he's gone?"

He nods. "Feels like a joke. Like he'll walk through the door any minute and tell me this was all just a way to get me here so we could get things back to how they used to be. And now..." He sighs. "He won't even get to meet his grandchildren, and they won't get to meet him. That's a real shame because he would've been the best grandfather."

I try to picture the Tim I met in Hawaii as *the best grandfather* and I'm having a hard time reconciling those two very different images.

"All my memories of my childhood are good ones," he says. "It was never me versus Jack back then. It was just one adventure after another for the three of us. It was bonding over a love of the same game. It was fishing and golfing and running marathons."

I press my lips together. "I'm so sorry, Luke."

He sits up. "I know. Let's try to get some rest. Tomorrow won't be easy."

He's right. I get ready for bed in the bathroom connecting this room to Jack's, and then I crawl under the covers. He goes after me, and he returns two minutes later.

"When was the last time you slept in this bed?" I ask once he joins me in bed.

"Right after I graduated college and before I moved to Vegas. Then I ran to Vegas and didn't look back."

We're both quiet and I lean over and press a kiss to his cheek in the dark room. "I love you," I whisper. "Whatever you need, I'm right here."

He clutches my hand in his. "Thank you," he whispers. "I love you, too."

CHAPTER 21

The room is empty when I roll over, and I check my phone. It's a little after eight, five our time. Luke emerges from the bathroom a minute later, and I'm thankful I don't have to navigate this house or his family alone.

"Good morning," he says softly.

"Morning," I say. I sit up. "You ready for this?"

He shrugs. "Nope. You?"

"I'm ready for whatever you need."

He presses his lips together. "Thank you."

"Can I take a quick shower?"

He nods. "I'll wait for you."

"You can go down," I say.

He shakes his head. "It's okay. Take your time."

I don't. I take a speed shower, make myself presentable, and when I emerge, I find Luke staring at that same photo he'd been studying last night.

He sets it down and glances up at me. "How are you so beautiful?" he asks.

Heat creeps into my cheeks. "Stop it," I say with a little smile.

He chuckles as he stands and walks over to me. He takes me into his arms and holds me a few beats, and I squeeze him back, like I'm transferring all the strength I have to him so he can navigate this day.

Carol and Kaylee are sitting together on the couch when we walk into the expansive family room. Their heads are bent together over a photo album, and Kaylee sniffles and wipes away a tear.

Carol doesn't express any emotions, and it's not the first time I see a bit of a resemblance between her and Luke. Normally he's pretty good at hiding what he's feeling, but he's been surprisingly open since he first got the call from Jack last night.

"Hey," Luke says tentatively as we walk into the room, and I can't imagine walking *tentatively* into a room holding my family members.

Kaylee stands and rushes to her brother's arms, and Carol remains seated. I study her for a quick beat as her eyes fall onto her children. She should feel a sense of pride there. Kaylee cries as Luke hugs her, and Carol should feel *some* sort of way about that. And I'm sure she does, but she's schooled herself not to show those feelings—just like she taught her son to.

Enter Ellie.

Between the way we feel about each other and the fact that we have a baby on the way plus everything in between, I've finally started to break down the walls Carol carefully constructed.

"Breakfast is in the kitchen," Carol says. She nods to the counter behind her, and I spot dishes and bowls in that direction through the open floor plan.

She doesn't have words of wisdom and she doesn't stand to hug her son. Instead, she remains stoic, and I finally start to see her for who she is. It must be the baby I'm carrying and the deep dive of my own mind into what sort of mother I want to be that helps me come to these realizations.

Or maybe it's some of Luke's late-night confessions whispered into the dark. Regardless of how she felt about him, or how he felt about her, they were still married for a long time and she just lost him.

Standing up to hug her son will fill her with emotion she isn't ready to handle...and maybe they're at a point where she isn't even sure a hug would be welcome. Maybe it wouldn't be, but the Luke I know is affectionate and loving. In this moment, he needs a hug from his mother, but she can't read that and he doesn't know how to tell her.

It comes down to a simple lack of communication.

Mentioning that food is in the kitchen is taking care of him in the way she knows how. She's doing the best she can under the circumstances as she's trying to navigate what she broke with her son, and I can only hope that she'll see over the next few days how much more he deserves. I can only hope that he'll forgive her and they can mend what's left so he doesn't have to go through this same sort of self-blame when eventually she joins her husband.

It's morbid to think that way, but it is what it is.

We find a spread of breakfast casseroles and danish on the counter, clearly the food of friends and neighbors who want to help but aren't sure how as the Dalton family reels from this shocking loss.

I grab some cheese danish and a slice of the casserole, as does Luke, and we stand at the counter separating the family room and the kitchen.

"What are you looking at?" Luke asks before he shoves in a forkful of casserole.

"Remember the Mexico trip when I was four?" Kaylee asks. "Because I don't, but you would've been a teenager."

Luke chuckles. "Yeah, I do. I was fourteen and Jack was fifteen and somehow he got his hands on a bottle of tequila. We got so sick and Dad was pissed."

I giggle at the thought of two teenaged boys getting wasted in Mexico on a family vacation, and Carol glances over at her son before pointedly saying, "I remember the dinner cruise and the markets downtown. I guess I blocked out the memory of my delinquent sons drinking underage."

Kaylee elbows her mom. "You were busy taking care of a little girl."

"A very active little girl who loved to climb everything to impress her brothers," Carol says, and she purses her lips.

"And we were always impressed with her climbing abilities," a deep voice says. I glance up and watch as Jack strides into the room. Even here in his family's home, even now under these circumstances, he holds this air of confidence and control.

"Jack!" Kaylee says, and she flies into his arms like she just did with Luke.

Kaylee proved where her loyalties lie when she told our secret at the wedding, but looking back, even I can see that she was just trying to protect her brother. And she should. That's what families do. As much as I hated it, hated *her* at the time, she only wanted what was best for her brother.

"Good morning everyone," he says.

Carol stands, but she doesn't move toward her son, and it's comforting to know that she doesn't fly toward Jack, either...that her parenting style is more of the *let them come to me* variety rather than choosing one son over the other.

Kaylee lets him go.

"Breakfast is in the kitchen," Carol repeats to Jack.

"Get over here, Mother," Jack says with affection, and unlike his little brother, he closes the gap between himself and his mother, who makes a small effort to move toward him as well. He pulls her into a hug and squeezes her tightly, and I watch this moment unfold as Carol's carefully crafted façade starts to crumble.

She sniffs and brushes a finger under her eye, and this is why she's been stoic. She doesn't want to lose it in front of her kids. She's putting herself in the lead position of this family now.

But letting each other in isn't just part of the process of grief. It's part of what makes a family *a family*.

And I suspect that by the time we're on the other side of the next few days, Luke's idea of family will transition once again.

CHAPTER 22

"How's the knee?" Jack joins us in the kitchen and circles the food, and I can't help but feel a little anxiety over what might happen between brothers. Will Jack brush his suspension and fine into the past given why they're standing in this room together?

"Getting better every day." Luke takes a bite of danish as we continue filling our plates.

"Glad to hear it."

"Still pissed Hammond didn't even get a flag for it," Luke says.

"I watched the tape, man." Jack shakes his head. "He should have. If it makes you feel any better, he got fined by the team."

"It doesn't," Luke says pointedly. He's out for the season, and Allen had to give up a few bucks. Doesn't really seem fair.

"And I gave him a shiner when I socked him one," Jack adds.

Luke chuckles. "Now *that* makes me feel a little better. You hit him?"

Jack adds a slice of casserole to a plate and grabs a fork. "And I told him he better not fuck with my little brother or I'd give him another black eye to match the first one."

When I glance up at Luke, his eyes are shining with a little bit of pride and maybe a little bit of admiration. It's plain to see these two care about each other, but they've let too many outside forces come between them.

If there's any sort of silver lining to the reason why we're here, maybe it's that it'll give these men some time to examine their relationship. Maybe they'll find a way to be as close as they once were.

And despite the fracture between Luke and the rest of them, I can't help but think that's something his father would have wanted.

Luke and I carry our plates over to the table, and Jack joins us a few beats later.

After a breakfast filled with meaningless small talk, we join Carol and Kaylee in the family room.

"What's that?" Jack asks.

"The album from our trip to Disney World when I was six," Kaylee says.

Jack sits beside Kaylee to flip through, and he chuckles at the first photo he sees. "Remember when Dad took us golfing?" he says to Luke.

Luke laughs. "We had to be sixteen and seventeen, right?"

Jack nods.

"It started *pouring* down rain, and the three of us got stuck in a flood on the course," Luke explains. "The golf cart died and we either had to abandon our golf bags with it or lug them as we waded through knee-deep water."

Jack laughs. "The lightning was crazy, and the clubhouse ended up sending out a little party bus to pick us up. When we got back to the hotel, the girls were getting manicures in the spa and didn't even know it had been raining."

Kaylee lets out a little giggle. "All I remember was the three of you were soaked and Mom just told you not to get the carpet all wet."

Carol purses her lips primly as she raises her brows. "Nobody likes a wet carpet."

I stifle another laugh, and they pull out another photo album while Luke flips through the Disney one beside me.

And that's pretty much how the day goes. Photo albums and memories with casserole and snacks peppered in. From all accounts, this seems like a picture-perfect happy family, though death isn't exactly when you bring up the bad times.

From what I can piece together, it seems the fracture started when Jack entered high school and really intensified around the time Jack went off to college. He was playing quarterback, and Tim was promoted to the quarterback coach at Michigan, and it just made sense that they'd bond over the position. Luke was cast aside for Jack, and maybe Tim thought Carol would pick up the slack there, but Carol had her hands full with a small girl at the time. Luke got good grades and stayed out of trouble, so he sort of fell off the radar.

After dinner, Jack asks the question it seems like everyone has been avoiding. "Do we need to start making arrangements?"

I'm doing the dishes just to do *something* to keep myself occupied, but I glance up at Carol. She's still sitting at the table with Jack and Kaylee. Luke excused himself from the room a few minutes ago, and I have no idea where he went.

"Bentley is taking care of it," she says. "I gave him your father's final wishes. It was all outlined in the will."

Bentley? Is there another brother I don't know about?

"Do you have the details yet?" Jack asks.

She shakes her head. "I told him you need to be back in Denver by Thursday."

"Thanks," Jack murmurs.

"He said he'd get back to me tonight."

Luke reappears just as I finish the dishes, and he's holding a stack of board games. "Look what I found," he says. He sets them in the middle of the kitchen table.

Carol lets out a small chuckle. "Your father *loved* game night," she says. "We haven't had one in years. Probably since you went off to college," she says to Kaylee.

"He's definitely the one who instilled a healthy sense of competition in us," Jack says.

"Monopoly, anyone?" Luke asks, and he opens the box.

Jack immediately grabs for the car, Luke goes for the shoe, and Kaylee takes the horse.

"Ellie?" Luke asks. "Want to play?"

"Sure," I say, and I slide into the seat beside him. I take the iron.

"Mom?" Kaylee asks.

She presses her lips together and allows the sides of her mouth to go up infinitesimally. "I'll just watch you for a bit."

"You sure?" Luke asks. "The thimble is still available." He holds it up and shakes it around, and she lets out the smallest grunt of a chuckle.

"You kids play," she says.

We get started, and it's actually quite a rousing game of Monopoly. It seems like Jack and Luke automatically team up against Kaylee first and then me once she's out. Carol watches her sons in silence as they team up to get me out.

"Your dad would be so proud seeing you two like this," she murmurs as it turns into a fierce competition between brothers.

A moment of silence passes over us all, and I breathe in what feels like peace in this room. It feels like the start of the mend.

After what seems like hours, Jack emerges the winner.

It seems like Jack is *always* the winner. From football to life to something as silly as a board game, he's a champion.

Carol's phone rings, so she bows out of the room for a few minutes, and she rejoins us just as Luke finishes cleaning up the play money from the game.

"That was Bentley," she says. "Your father didn't want a wake. He wanted a simple church funeral with a brunch afterward since it was his favorite meal. The funeral is tomorrow at nine with the burial at the cemetery following. We'll head to the restaurant immediately after that. Bentley will meet us back here after that to read the will."

"Tomorrow?" Kaylee asks. "So soon?" Her eyes sparkle with unshed tears as she glances around at her family, and I'm reminded how the annual family trips were her idea, her way of seeing her entire family together despite the rifts between them. "We don't even get another day together like this?"

Carol presses her lips together. "You're all free to return home after the funeral, or you can stay as long as you'd like. It's your choice." She turns and heads out of the room, and I assume it's because Kaylee's question triggered something in her. She had to run out because God forbid she shows even a shred of emotion in front of her children.

I wonder what sort of healing powers her tears would have for her and for everyone in this room. I wonder how powerful it would be for them to see how hurt she is by this.

That's not her, and from what I can gather, it's never been her.

But it's never too late to change.

The three siblings share more memories around the kitchen table, and as much as Luke will say he did it for his sister, I can see it in his eyes. He needs this, too. He needs his family, especially in a time like this. Luke never spoke about wanting to fix things with his family until he got the call that it was too late to patch up his relationship with his father, but I can see it in his eyes.

He's grateful for these tiny moments with his family.

It's a breakthrough.

CHAPTER 23

Kaylee heads to bed next, which leaves Luke and me with Jack.

"You're playing the Cowboys this weekend?" Luke asks.

Jack nods. "I studied film on the plane and Coach is sending me some plays to go over on the plane home."

"I'm glad Bentley arranged the funeral for tomorrow," Luke says.

"Who's Bentley?" I finally ask.

"The family lawyer," Luke and Jack say at the same time.

"Ah," I say, nodding. Of course the Daltons have a family lawyer. There's a lot about this life I'm still learning, I guess.

"I'm glad, too," Jack says. "I love what I do, but missing my own father's funeral to play a game would've been..."

"Tough," Luke finishes. "But if anyone in the world would've understood that, it's Dad."

Jack huffs out a chuckle. "Yeah, he's the one that instilled my work ethic, that's for sure. And he's the one who taught me that you don't have a choice in this career a lot of times."

"It's all part of it," Luke murmurs. "You have to take the good with the bad, I guess."

"What should we do about Mom?" Jack asks, changing the subject suddenly.

Luke raises a brow. "I was wondering the same."

I'm in the dark. What do they even mean?

"I'd think she'd want to be near her grandchild," Luke adds, and I assume he means Jack's kid.

Jack nods. "But she'd hate the weather in Denver. She always talked about how much she hated it here in Michigan."

"You think I should ask her if she wants to come to Vegas?" Luke asks.

Whoa, whoa, whoa.

Hold the phone.

Is he serious?

Carol...in Vegas?

That's a hard no from this camp. I think it might be an even worse idea than Michelle living with us.

Jack twists his lips. "No grandchildren there," he points out.

"Um," Luke says, and he glances at me. My eyes widen, and Jack clings onto that.

"You're not..." he says, his eyes on me.

My eyes meet Luke's, and he nods.

"I am," I say.

Jack whistles then shakes his head. "Wow. I guess you were serious when you said this wasn't just for show."

Luke chuckles. "Admittedly that's how it began." His honesty is shocking, and it sends a dart of anxiety through my chest. But then he reaches over and takes my hand in his, and somehow that manages to calm every fear inside. "But that's not where we're at now."

"Congratulations," Jack says. He glances at our joined hands. "Looks like you won this round."

Luke's brows dip down. "What do you mean?"

He studies us. "You seem good for each other." He blows out a breath. "I thought about trying with Michelle since we're having a kid, but, Jesus Christ, how did you put up with her for as long as you did?"

I can't help my snort-laugh at that.

"I was blessed with a lot more patience than you," Luke says. "Plus I drank a fuck ton of whiskey to get through it."

Jack laughs. "I don't drink in season," he admits. "Except for special occasions." He stands and walks over to the enormous walk-in pantry, and he returns a moment later with a bottle of Macallan and two short tumblers. "You okay to have some?" he asks Luke.

Luke stares at the bottle for a few beats before his eyes meet his brother's, and then he nods without a word.

"I take it this bottle has some special meaning?" I ask as Jack uncaps the bottle and pours two short glasses with no ice.

"The Rolls Royce of single malts," Luke and Jack say at the same time.

Luke grunts a soft chuckle. "Our dad loved a good single malt scotch, and that's what he always said about this one. His dad gave him a bottle when my parents got married and told him it was only for special occasions. So he had a glass the night Jack was born, and me and Kaylee, too. He had one the night Jack got into USC, and the night I got into Wisconsin."

"Not always the happy occasions, either," Jack says. "Just the big life events. When Uncle Larry died, he had some. After grandpa's funeral, and grandma's, too."

Luke nods. "Our cousin Jackie's wedding."

"When we won the state game in high school," Jack adds.

"When you were drafted," Luke says.

Jack nods. "And when you were."

"At your wedding?" I ask Luke, and he shakes his head.

"No, not that night. At least not that I know of." He glances at Jack then down at the glass sitting untouched in front of him. "I think he knew it wasn't going to last. I think that's just a small part of why he was so hard on me."

"He was hard on you because he loved you," Jack says softly.

Luke keeps his eyes down on his glass. "He had a funny way of showing it."

"Be that as it may, he talked to me a lot about how you were your own man. He always thought you'd take flight away from my spotlight. He didn't know how to coach a receiver like he could a quarterback, so that naturally pushed us together." His voice seems to get a little emotional, and seeing his carefully crafted exterior start to crack causes *me* to get a little emotional, too. I swipe away a tear.

"I know you always thought he pawned you off on Coach Sterling," Jack continues, "but he did it because he thought you had the best chance at becoming pro with someone else's help. He couldn't provide that for you, so he got someone who could. He gave you space to thrive on your own away from me."

Luke's eyes seem to mist over a little, but he keeps his face down to hide it. I can't help but wonder how these revelations make him feel. A little better about their relationship? Or even worse that he can't fix it now—that it's too late to get the actual truth from his dad's mouth?

Jack clears his throat then holds up his glass. "To Dad."

Luke sighs heavily, but then he picks up his glass too. He taps it to Jack's with a *clink*. "To Dad," he repeats.

I get the sudden feeling like these two men have a lot more to talk about, so I head up to bed.

I don't know how much time passes, but I wake when the bed dips as he gets in. "You doing okay?" I ask into the darkness.

"Yeah," he says softly. He leans over and presses a kiss to my lips. "Tonight was..." He trails off as he searches for the right word. "Healing, I think. For Jack and me. It felt like old times, laughing and talking about the past. Drinking Dad's Macallan. He told me he's happy for you and me, and we talked more about Michelle and how he feels about the baby. We needed it." He sniffs.

I reach over and pull him into me. I hold him until his breathing evens out, and then we sleep in each other's arms. Tonight was healing, and tomorrow will be difficult, as will the days that follow...but my last thought before I drift to sleep is that through this tragedy, Luke just might have gotten his brother back.

CHAPTER 24

I remain close to Luke's side throughout the morning as we attend the funeral, where we sit in the first row as we listen to a preacher read words from the Bible that are supposed to provide comfort to those gathered. I spot my brother and Nicki toward the back of the church, and I'm so thankful for the friendship he and Luke have formed. I'm thankful he's here for Luke. I see Coach Thompson and Mo sitting near Josh. It's another relationship of Luke's I'm grateful for.

I part from Luke long enough for him and Jack to join some other men I don't know as they work as pallbearers. I hold his hand as we travel with Jack, Kaylee, and Carol to the cemetery, where we watch the casket as it's lowered into the plot.

And it's there, after the preacher is long gone and friends have dispersed to the restaurant for brunch and the immediate family of Daltons is all that remains, when Luke breaks the silence as they all stare at the casket.

"Life's too damn short for all this anger between us."

Nobody moves for a beat. Nobody says a word.

But then Carol speaks. "You're right," she says softly.

She doesn't apologize for the way she's treated any of them, but just the admission that she agrees with her son seems like a huge leap in a new direction. And maybe in a few days they'll each get back to their own lives and go on living the way they have been. On the other hand, this could be the wake-up call they all needed.

I've already seen a change between Luke and Jack.

They can be competitors on the field and brothers off it, but it seems like somewhere along the line, they lost that brotherhood.

Carol turns toward Luke, and I let go of his hand as I urge him toward his mother. She hugs him, and he clings to her, and both of them shake with silent tears. Kaylee's tears are a little louder as she sniffs, and even Jack seems to get emotional. He hides it by hugging his mother from the other side, sandwiching her between her sons. Kaylee hugs Luke from behind, too, and while this moment doesn't fix *everything*, it does go a long way to mend what was so broken for so long.

Luke introduces me as his wife to family and friends whose names I'll never remember. I spend a little time with my brother and Nicki, but mostly I stick by Luke's side in case he needs anything.

We're asked a thousand times why we didn't have a big wedding, and I realize that these are all people who care about Luke. I have the same network of family and friends of my own who also missed out on things, and now that we've transitioned from *fake* to *real*, I'm starting to feel the sting of what I missed out on.

I always dreamed of the big fairy tale wedding. The dress. The shoes. The hair. The tiara. The veil. And most of all, celebrating the love I share with the man of my dreams as we seal our commitment in front of everyone who matters to us.

I didn't get that. Neither of us did.

I think it's time to revisit the idea of a wedding. It might be a little late, and I might be a little knocked up, but it's something I didn't realize I wanted as badly as I do until we were reminded over and over today that we never had it.

After brunch, we head back to the home where Luke grew up. Bentley is waiting in the office when we arrive, and it's time for the reading of the will.

"This is for family only," Bentley says, and he glances at me.

"Ellie's my wife," Luke says, his hand tightening around mine.

I sit between Luke and Jack on the black leather couch. Carol and Kaylee chose the plush chairs facing the desk, and Bentley slides into the executive chair behind the desk.

"First and foremost, let me express my condolences," Bentley says. "You lost a husband and a father, and I lost my best friend. I'm devastated, but I'm glad to be here to carry out Tim's final wishes. As you know, he did well for many years as an investment banker, and he gave up that career to coach football. His knowhow in the field of investments left him with a rather large sum." He turns to Carol. "You're the main beneficiary. You'll keep the house, and you have enough investments and assets to live more than comfortably for the rest of your life. Only a portion of Tim's net worth, which is a rather healthy sum, will be split amongst Tim's three children provided they meet certain conditions."

"Conditions?" Kaylee repeats.

Bentley nods. "Tim provided for you when he was alive, but in his death, he wanted to ensure you met certain criteria in order to receive an inheritance in the sum of ten million dollars each. These are simple requests that are meant to encourage you to take the path he thought you'd be happiest going down. We'll start with you, Kaylee." He puts on his readers and glances at a paper in his hand. "You will receive your sum upon earning your degree at your graduation. Your father wanted you to use the money to buy a house and get started on your adult life as you begin your first career in a field he hopes you love."

He glances at Jack next. "Jack, you'll receive your sum after you've been married for one year." Jack snorts with derision beside me. "Your father had high hopes that you'd settle down and find someone who could both put up with and take care of you, and he felt that a year would be long enough to seal your commitment."

And then he looks at Luke. Anxiety pulses in my chest. "Finally, Luke. Your father recently amended your condition. Initially, you and Jack had the same stipulation. But when he saw you marry someone you hardly knew with the accusation that you were only planning to be married to her for a year, he had concerns that you knew about this provision of his will."

Luke shakes his head. "I don't care about the damn money," he says. "I have my own. And I had no idea about his conditions."

Bentley looks sternly at Luke. "Shall I continue?"

"By all means," Luke says snidely.

Bentley clears his throat and reads from another paper. "This is from an email your father sent to me. 'Because I want my sons both to experience the joy of fatherhood and I'm not sure whether his marriage is real, Luke will now receive his sum after the birth of his first child. He will be an incredible father, more than I ever was to him, and while I know he can and will provide for his family, I never want him to worry about their futures. I ask that he either use this money for his family or, if he doesn't want my money, which I would certainly understand, that his portion is donated to the charity he recently started.'"

Luke keeps his eyes trained to the ground.

Is this when we're supposed to tell everyone gathered that I'm actually currently growing that first child? That Luke's inheritance is a mere six months away?

"As you can all see, these are simple conditions made in the interest of the kind of life he thought you each wanted from what he knew of you. And I think he knew you all better than you gave him credit for." He looks around at everyone gathered as he speaks until he gets to that last sentence, when his eyes train on Luke. "I'm the executor of the will, and as soon as you have met the conditions, please call me and we'll immediately start the transfer."

Bentley excuses himself after no one in the room has further questions, and Carol walks him out. When she returns, the four of us are still sitting silently in the office as each of the siblings works through their own reaction to their individual conditions.

"He knew exactly what I wanted," Kaylee says to her mother through her tears. "Exactly what I *needed* to start my life."

"I'm not really sure he knew me at all," Jack says, a hint of surprise in his tone. "I don't want to get married."

"Ellie's pregnant," Luke murmurs.

CHAPTER 25

"She's what?" Carol asks.

"Pregnant," Luke repeats.

"Oh, Lord," Carol mutters. "Are we absolutely sure it's yours?"

If we didn't just go through the same thing with Michelle and if I was a little less understanding of Carol's personality, I'd be totally insulted by that comment.

But this is the Dalton family. That's all the explanation necessary to see that her question makes perfect sense.

"We are one hundred percent sure," I say pointedly. "No other possibilities." I nearly go so far as to say he's the only man I've had sex with since Todd dumped me back in May, but I leave that part out.

Carol stares at Luke for a few beats, and then her eyes edge over to me. I see the skepticism written on her face, and Luke must catch onto it as well.

"This is real, Mom," he says. He glances at me, and I nod. He grabs for my hand. "It didn't start out that way. It started as a way to get Michelle off my back." He glances at Jack, who nods his encouragement for Luke to continue. "But something changed along the way, and Ellie is the woman I'm going to spend my life with. I've never been with someone who put me first. Who cared about me more than herself. Who cared about my future more than my present."

He says the last part thickly, and it's a stark reminder that both Savannah and Michelle and probably countless others cared more about the fact that he's a pro football player than anything else. And that strikes me as incredibly sad.

I've gotten to know the man beneath the shoulder pads over the last few months, and he's a star in more ways than just on the field. Simply put, he's the Prince Charming I've been searching for.

And I'm glad for his past relationships. They helped make him into the man sitting beside me right now. The man I love.

"She takes care of me," he says. "She changed my bandages after my surgery and she makes sure I'm doing my exercises. She keeps up my social media and makes sure fans know I'm okay. She loves me fiercely, and she's taking such good care of the baby by eating right and learning everything she can. She's not just the woman I love. She's the best friend I've ever had, and she's going to be a phenomenal mother to our lucky children."

My eyes fill with tears at his words, and I squeeze his hand. He turns toward me, and I mouth *I love you* to him. He squeezes my hand back.

Carol raises a brow, and the room is quiet as everyone awaits her response expectantly. And instead of congratulating her son for finding the love of his life and on the upcoming birth of his first child, she stands and walks out of the room without a word. The door clicks shut behind her, and we all sit in stunned silence for a second.

Heat creeps up my back as anger sparks deep inside and explodes through every nerve ending in my body.

Is she freaking serious?

Hell no, lady.

I don't care if she's my mother-in-law. You don't respond to your son's bleeding-heart confession by walking out of the room without a word. You don't respond to your son's words that his wife is pregnant with silence.

I may be starting to understand the Dalton family, but what she just did isn't okay.

I stand as heat pricks behind my eyes. My fists are clenched as I walk toward the door. I think Luke says something, a feeble attempt to try to stop me probably, and maybe Jack and Kaylee say something too...but the rushing in my head prevents any of their words from registering.

I'm going to give Carol a piece of my mind, and I move with speed before I can change my mind and before anyone can stop me.

I throw open the door, and I open it with such force that it bounces back against the spring doorstop and slams shut behind me again.

I find Carol standing in the hallway a few steps away from the office. She faces away from the door.

"You have nothing to say to your son?" I ask, my voice full of venom.

She doesn't turn around. She doesn't even acknowledge that I spoke.

But through my red haze of anger, I see her shoulders shaking. She sniffs as she finally turns around, and her hand is over her mouth as she cries into it. Her eyes are red as tears stream down her cheeks.

"Thank you," she whispers. She brushes the tears away. "For taking care of my son. For being everything he needs."

Understanding dawns on me. She ran out so nobody would see her like this. I'm sure I'm the last person she wants to cry in front of, and yet somehow it must be better than crying in front of her children.

The tender heart in me can't stand to see anyone crying, so it's natural as I move toward her and open my arms for a hug.

I'm surprised when she moves her hand from her face and moves into my arms, and I hold her for a beat as she lets out the pent-up emotions she tries so hard to hide from everybody.

"This is hard," I say softly. "It's okay to let your kids see that you're struggling."

She seems to pull herself together at my words. "No, it's not," she says, moving out of my arms. She sniffs again and wipes her cheeks with her fingertips. "They need to know they can come to me with anything and I'm strong enough to handle it."

I shake my head. "They need to know you're human. They need to see that you have emotions, too, and that it's okay to express them. Luke *still* has a hard time showing me what he's feeling. He learned that from you. I don't want either of you to feel like you have to hide what's inside because you know what?" I hold my hands out wide. "There's more room out here than in there." I point to her chest at the end.

She sighs. "It's just not who I am."

I shake my head. "But it's okay to run out of a room when your son finally opens up to you?"

She presses her lips together. "I'm just so happy for him. He's doing well despite everything we did to mess him up."

"You didn't mess him up," I say. "He's a wonderful man, and you'd know that if you bothered to get to know him."

She stares at me a beat, and nerves rattle around inside until she speaks. "He's right, you know," she says. My brows dip because I don't know what she means. "You're going to make a wonderful mother."

She leaves the hallway with those words, and now it's my turn to cry by myself for a minute.

CHAPTER 26

Jack stands on the top rung of a ladder in the front hall while Luke hands him a replacement bulb for the one burned out in the chandelier.

"How pissed would the Broncos organization be if I accidentally tipped over the ladder while you're on top?" Luke teases.

"At least I can get on a ladder," Jack retorts.

"Too soon," Luke says, laughing as he shakes his head.

I'm still making him do his exercises while we're here in Michigan. Most of his therapy has transitioned to home care at this point, anyway. He still has a limp, and his knee isn't strong yet, but he's getting better and better every day. His next appointment with the doctor is in a week, and I'm interested to hear what the team trainers have to say about Luke's potential for next season. I'm also interested to hear what Calvin might say.

"What else, Mom?" Jack asks.

"I told you I can hire someone to do that stuff, boys," she says, her tone one of scolding but her expression one of pride.

"Why hire someone when we're right here to do it?" Luke asks, and Jack nods.

It's funny seeing Jack and Luke team up this way. They both want to do little odds and ends around the house. They both want to make life a little easier for their mom. They're working together after working against each other for so many years.

It feels like it's been a long time in the making, and if it feels this good for me, I can't imagine how it feels for Luke and Jack.

The men go through their dad's closet together. Carol pops in to check on them, but mostly they take care of it both so Carol doesn't have to and also so they have time together to dig up old memories. They each keep a few items that are meaningful to them, and Kaylee walks away with some mementos as well.

I sort of wonder how Jack feels about that money. Luke indicated that he doesn't care about it. He said he has his own, and Jack does, too. But that doesn't change the fact that I'm grateful the money will be set aside for our kids. Luke may have plenty, but it's comforting to know we have insurance should anything go wrong between the two of us. I don't anticipate it will, but we have no idea what the future may hold—just like we had no idea he'd take a hit that ended his entire season and potentially his career.

Jack takes a call from Michelle later in the evening, and we can all hear her bitching about being pregnant over the phone. He rolls his eyes and heads upstairs to talk privately, and once we all hear the door click shut to Jack's room, it's Carol who speaks up first. "There are two types of pregnant women. The miserable ones who hate being pregnant," she says, glancing upstairs to indicate Michelle, and then her eyes land on me. "And the glowing ones who seem to have it all together."

Did Carol just...dare I say...*compliment* me?

Kaylee loses it to a fit of giggles at her mom's words, and I can't help my *glowing* smile.

Later in the evening, we're all sitting together in the family room when Luke looks at his mother. "What do you need this big old mansion for?"

She lifts a shoulder. "It's been home for a lot of years."

"It doesn't have to be home forever, though," Luke says. He glances at me, and as much as I still think this is a bad idea, that moment in the hallway earlier today was a breakthrough for Carol and me. I think I'm learning how to deal with her. It seems like I earned her respect when I stood up to her by standing up for her son, and I guess that's what every parent wants for their child, isn't it? Someone to love them so much that they'll stand up to the scariest monsters to defend them.

"Move to Vegas," Luke says, and Kaylee gasps. "You can get to know your grandchild, and Ellie, and even me. We'd love to have you close by."

I have to admit, I appreciate that he said *close by* and not *in our house*...but *love* is a little strong.

She glances around. "Oh, Luke," she says softly. "I don't know. There are so many happy memories here. And, I guess, not so happy ones as well, but that's what makes it a home, doesn't it?"

"Like when Jack jumped over the bannister?" Luke says, nodding upstairs to the bannister in the hallway that overlooks the family room.

Carol purses her lips. "Oh, you mean when he sprained his ankle and couldn't play baseball?"

Jack shrugs innocently. "Or like when Luke hit the mailbox with a baseball bat?"

"How about the time you walked in on Jack *naked* on the couch with Sandi Meyer?" Luke counters.

Not to be outdone, Jack adds, "How about the time you caught Luke in *your bed* with Jamie Keck?"

I turn to Luke with a raised brow, and he looks like he wants to kill Jack. Really, Luke? In your *parents'* bed? Does it get grosser than that?

Kaylee turns red and Carol shakes her head. "Always one adventure after another with you two," Carol mutters, and I giggle.

"Just think about it," Luke says to Carol, getting back to the point of the conversation.

She nods. "I'll think about it."

They may not be perfect, but this is certainly what families are made of. I think back to our time in Hawaii when I was so certain I wasn't meant to be a part of the Dalton family.

I wasn't—not *that* family, anyway. Not the one with hurt and pain and scars between them. They're still there, and they always will be, but it feels like Luke has jump over a lot of hurdles to finally find a place where he can be close to his family again. It's unfortunate that it took a tragedy to get here, but I've learned that tragedies have the power to birth wonderful things.

So I'm part of the Dalton clan now.

It feels good. It feels right.

And I'm so excited to start my own little family with my Prince Charming.

* * *

"I want to redo my will when we get home," he says as we settle onto chairs in the first-class lounge at the airport.

"Oh?" I ask. These are exactly the necessary types of morbid conversations I dread.

"You're carrying my child. You're my wife. You and the baby deserve it all if anything happens to me."

"That's nice of you to say, Luke, but nothing's going to happen to you." My tone is adamant. I can't have anything happen to him. I can't even imagine my life without him.

"What happened with my dad...it just goes to show that you never know. He was here one minute and gone the next, and it was totally unexpected." Tears fill my eyes as he talks because he's absolutely right. We never know what tomorrow will bring...if we're lucky enough to have a tomorrow. "I want to be prepared if the worst should ever happen. It's just insurance," he says, and he squeezes my hand.

"Whatever you want," I say. It's such a weird conversation to have. He earned everything he has well before he met me...and yet he wants me to have it all if anything ever happens to him.

"Whatever *we* want," he amends. "It's yours now anyway. I'm going to have Greg create some new paperwork for us if that's okay with you."

"I don't want to talk about this stuff," I say.

"I know." He rubs my leg over my jeans, and I'm glad we're headed for home because the button on these things barely clasped this morning and I think it's about time to start shopping for maternity clothes. "But they're the type of grown-up conversations we need to have."

"I know you're right, but the thought that something could happen to either of us...I just can't think about it. Not with a baby on the way. All I can think about is a future with us holding hands as we stare down at him with all the love in the world."

"That's all I want, too." He leans over and presses a soft kiss to my lips as he sets his big hand over my stomach. It's just starting to bloat a little before the big swell comes, and I can't wait for every moment that lies ahead. "I want to live life to the fullest because we don't have any guarantees that we'll get a tomorrow."

"In that same vein," I say, finally just going for it, "I want to have a wedding. A real one. Call it a renewal or whatever, but I want a ceremony, and I want a party, and I want my friends and family there as well as yours. I want to celebrate this love we share with everyone important to us before the life we created arrives."

"Then you'll have one," he says, and his words are so simple that I feel like I could ask him to reach up and grab the moon for me and he'd do everything in his power to grasp it. "Start planning, or hire someone, and just tell me what you need me to do."

"Show up and wear the tux I pick out for you," I say, and he chuckles.

"Consider it done, wife."

I smile at his endearment. "I like when you call me that, husband."

He grins at me. "It's really starting to feel like it, isn't it?"

I nod. "Just wait until this baby gets here. Then our lives will be flipped upside down once again."

He squeezes my hand again. "I can't wait."

CHAPTER 27

"I think I'm ready to talk about what comes next."

His words whispered in the dark when we're back home in our own bed come as a shock. We both fell under the covers with exhaustion once I emptied the suitcases and separated the laundry, and I assumed I'd be drifting to sleep after a quick kiss goodnight.

But his words wake me with a start.

"You are?" I ask on a gasp.

"I've been thinking a lot about it over the last few days. I know I said it was bad luck to talk about the future, but I haven't really had a string of good luck lately despite my best efforts to fill myself with good luck charms."

"Good luck charms?" I repeat. "You mean...Lucky Charms?"

He chuckles. "You figured me out. My grandfather nicknamed me Lucky Luke because of the copious amounts of Lucky Charms I ate as a kid."

I giggle. "That clearly carried over to adulthood."

"It gives me that warm, comforting feeling of childhood every time I pour a bowl. So, yeah, it carried over, and I'm not embarrassed by that."

"You shouldn't be." I reach over and squeeze his arm. "I think it's one of the most endearing things about you."

"You know what's one of the most endearing things about *you*?" he asks.

"Hm?" I murmur.

"Your tits."

I smack him in the arm, and he laughs.

"I was nearly asleep when you started this conversation by saying you wanted to talk about the future," I remind him. "You're not getting out of that by seducing me, so get talking, Dalton."

"Yes ma'am." He sighs. "I keep thinking about what happens next if I *can't* play. It's a real possibility. I'm working hard, and my knee is doing better, and I want it...but there are no guarantees I'll wind up with a contract on the other side of this. So I've been thinking over my options."

"And what conclusions have you come to?" I ask.

"This all hangs on my recovery, obviously, so I don't have a timeline...but I was thinking I could coach."

"You'd make an incredible coach," I say. It's a relief to hear that he wants to coach—and not because it means he'll still be a part of the game he loves so much, but because it's a decision. It's a future.

"Thank you. But I don't think that's what I want."

His words shake my relief. "It's not?"

I think he shakes his head, but it's dark in here so I'm not sure. "No. I think I'd love it, but I think there are other ways to still be involved with the game that I'd love more."

"Like what?"

"Big life changes mean big priority changes," he begins.

"Such as..." I trail off and wait for him to fill in the blank.

"Such as *you*. I've never loved a woman more than I love the game. But then I met you."

Tears fill my eyes at his words.

"You flipped my entire world upside down, Ellie, and I love it. I love *you*. I want to be around for you and the baby."

"Luke..." I say, the tears in my eyes splashing over as my chest tightens with love. "I love you, too." My words are whispered through the emotion clogging my throat.

God, I love him.

I turn in toward him and I kiss him. He welcomes me into his arms as he deepens the kiss and pulls me against him. He flips me so I'm on my back and he's hovering over me, and I know we're in the middle of an important conversation, but somehow this seems to be a part of it. I want to know what he wants next out of life, but I also want to feel his body as he enters mine. We can talk later. For now, our bodies will do the talking.

He's different as he kisses me. His focus is fully on me—and it's always been there, but he had things holding him back. The game, or the injury, or his own personality where hiding his emotions was ingrained by his parents. But if the last few days taught us anything, it's that he never has to hide from me.

Our clothes fly in different directions, and he flips us again so I end up on top of him so he can rest his leg. It's dark in here, but there's enough light from the moon edging in around the sides of the curtains that I can see where he is. He reaches up and caresses my breasts as I lower down onto him, both of us moaning at the now-familiar feel of nothing between us as I begin to move. I reach down and stroke my own clit as he moves in and out of me, our bodies rocking together in a perfect rhythm that I don't think I'll ever get enough of. He bats my hand out of the way and takes over my clit, and the way he knows exactly how to handle my body sends me into a mind-blowing, earth-shattering climax far too soon.

He follows soon after, growling his way through an epic release as my body milks his, and when it's all over, I lean down to kiss him while he's still inside me, love and lust and satisfaction all swirling thickly around us. He holds the back of my head for a few beats as he deepens our kiss, and there's one thing I know for certain. I will never, ever get tired of kissing this man.

Once we've both cleaned up and returned to bed, he picks up our conversation where we left it off.

"As I was saying before you came onto me—" he begins, and I interrupt him.

"Um, excuse me? *You* came onto *me*."

He snort-laughs. "Hardly. You turned into me and sent off all the signals!"

"Whatever!" I tease him. "You totally kissed me first!"

He laughs. "Well, I got mine and you got yours." He laces his fingers through mine beneath the covers.

"Truth. That was a good one."

"It was. But with you, they're all good ones."

He leans over for a kiss, and before our lips connect, I say, "Let it be noted that *you* are the one starting it this time."

He laughs and nips my lips with his. "As I was saying before, I want to be here for all his milestones, and I want to celebrate them with you. Combine that with your passion for public relations, and I started dreaming up some different possibilities."

"Possibilities?" I echo.

"What would you say about working together?"

My brows dip. "Working together on what?"

"I have two ideas, and I'd like your opinion on both."

"Go for it." What I really want to say is that he just knocked every last bit of energy right out of me and I'm ready to fall into sleep now, but he sounds so excited that I don't have the heart to say it.

"Well, for one thing, we could run our charity together," he says. "And for another...I'm thinking about starting up my own sports agency to run alongside Prince Charming Public

Relations. You could be the publicist for my clients and we could work hand-in-hand to secure endorsements and negotiate contracts."

"Oh, Luke," I say. "I love the idea. But I don't know anything about sports. I already feel like I'm struggling with my clients, and I'd be terrified of letting you down."

"Enter Luke," he says.

CHAPTER 28

"Your knee is making excellent progress," Dr. Charles says at Luke's two-month post-surgery checkup a couple weeks later. "How has it been feeling?"

"A little pain when I take stairs or try to walk for more than a few minutes," Luke admits.

"There's still some mild swelling. Have you been icing?" the doctor asks.

Luke shakes his head. "I've been doing the exercises, though." He points a thumb in my direction. "She makes me."

"Good work," Dr. Charles says, nodding toward me. "Ice it three to four times a day for twenty minutes. The swelling is very mild but that will likely eradicate it. Keep doing those exercises. It'll help with your range of motion, and the harder you work on it now, the quicker we'll see you back on the field. But take it easy, too. No running. No marathons. We'll get there."

"Thank you, Doctor," I say. He leaves after he makes sure we have no further questions. When we get home, a large box sits in the entryway.

"What's that?" I ask.

Luke grins. "Open it and find out."

"What have you done now?" I ask, narrowing my eyes at him.

He just shrugs innocently.

I tear the tape off the cardboard and flip open the box. "Clothes?" I ask. I pull out tops with plenty of room and jeans with tan belly bands around the waist and panties and bras and pajamas.

"Maternity," he says. "You've been saying for two weeks that you want to get some maternity clothes, and I had Debbie help me figure out what to order when you cried the other night that you could no longer get your jeans to button."

I laugh at the memory as I shake my head. "Man, the emotions are *strong* sometimes." I look at the box again and my eyes fill. I swipe away an escaped tear, and he chuckles. "Thank you. This is so kind of you."

He reaches for me and pulls me into his arms as he thumbs away another tear that tipped over. "You've taken such good care of me, Ellie. It's the least I can do to try to pay that back."

"It's not about being even or paying back. I take care of you because I love you."

He presses a soft kiss to my forehead. "Right back at you."

I melt into a puddle right there, and I'm trying to pull myself together again when the doorbell rings. We're both still standing in the foyer.

"Are you expecting anybody?" he asks.

I shake my head. "It's probably Josh stopping by to see how your appointment went."

"I bet you're right," he says, and he moves toward the door and tosses it open as I sink down into the pile of clothes as I hold up a gorgeous white sweater made out of the softest material.

I wait to hear my brother's voice, but instead I hear Luke say, "Mom?"

Mom?

Carol?

What the hell is she doing here?

"Hi," she says, and her voice sounds tentative. Carol Dalton has never been tentative about anything a day in her life.

"Come on in," he says, opening the door wider.

She glances down at me in my pile of clothes as she walks in. "Am I interrupting something?"

I giggle. "Your son just surprised me with all this. He is just the sweetest, most wonderful man in the world."

Luke looks embarrassed, and Carol looks proud. "How kind," she says.

"Mom, what are you doing here?"

"Don't I get a hug first?" she asks, and I almost laugh at the question. She's *never* started a greeting with a hug.

It's been three weeks since we last saw her, and I study her as her son wraps his arms around her. She looks tired. Worn down. Defeated.

Different.

I hug her next even though she didn't ask for one. She seems like she could use one anyway...maybe I could, too.

"Can I get you something to drink?" I ask.

"Some water would be lovely," she says.

"Of course. Come on in." I pile the clothes back into the box and head to the kitchen.

"So...are you going to tell us what you're doing here?" Luke asks once we're sitting around the kitchen table.

She clears her throat. "I thought a lot about what you said, about how I don't need that big old house all to myself, and you're right. I don't. All my friends in Michigan came by way of your father's job. Everything there reminds me of him. Every corner I turn, I see mistakes I made. And now it's too late to change them, but it's not too late to change other things, to fix other mistakes."

She pauses, and my chest tightens. Is she moving here? In with us? Can I even handle that?

No. The answer would be no.

I love Luke, and I want him to thrive and to succeed. I don't want him to be pulled down by the weight of his past and the mistakes of his family, and I'm terrified this will only lead to disappointment all the way around. People don't *really* change. Some tragedy happens, and everyone acts differently for a little while, but then things go back to the way they were. That's just life.

"I'm moving to Las Vegas...if you'll still have me," she says, and my heart drops into my stomach.

I school my expression to blank, but I'm not sure how successful I am in keeping the horror off my face.

"Of course we'll have you, Mom," Luke says. "You're welcome to stay here a while if you need to. Right, Ellie?"

I nod as I'm supposed to. "Of course," I murmur.

Carol glances at me. Gone is the look like I'm some annoying nuisance, and at least that is a small comfort. At least maybe now she realizes I'm sticking around.

I try to look at the bright side. My parents have already moved here, she's moving here, and we'll have people fighting over who gets to babysit when we want a date night. I'm sure we won't feel smothered at all after living without our parents this close for so damn long.

Right. And if I keep telling myself that, maybe I'll start to believe it.

I shake off the selfishness I'm feeling. I want Luke all to myself, but that's not reasonable or possible. He deserves this second chance with his mother—*if* she has truly changed and is ready to make amends.

Either way, whatever happens, I'll stand by his side and hold his hand.

"I put the house up for sale last week," she says softly. "I went to Denver to visit with Jack. I've talked to Kaylee every day. But something is calling me here." She pauses and focuses on her son. "I'd like to get to know you and your wife. I can't wait to meet your baby. I think Jack will need my help more than you will when it comes to the babies, but I don't know where that baby will be. Could be right here in Vegas since this is where Michelle is based." Her eyes edge to me. "I don't want to be a burden to either of you, but I'd like to try to make up for some of our lost time."

Luke reaches across the table to take her hand in his. "I'd love that, Mom," he says.

My tight chest seems to loosen at his words. If he'd love it, then I will, too. "We both would," I echo.

She nods once. "Thank you both," she says, and she seems to shift back to the prim woman I first met. Then she seems to think twice about it and she thaws a little. "I'm looking at some houses today if you'd like to come with."

"I have a meeting with one of my coaches in a bit," Luke says. "I'm so sorry."

I have a stack of paperwork to go through, a take two wedding to plan, and about four hundred emails to go through, but I guess it all can wait. "I'd love to go," I say.

After all, the sooner we find her a place of her own, the sooner I can stop worrying that she'll want to move in with us.

CHAPTER 29

They say the second trimester is like a vacation, sandwiched between the exhaustion of the first and the discomfort of the third. I don't know if I'd call this a vacation, exactly, but I feel good. Most of the time.

I'm finally starting to show a little, and I'm thankful every day for the clothes Luke ordered for me since my waistline is expanding. And it's with that in mind that I approach my husband with a very important question. I find him on the couch with his knee elevated and ice on it.

"When should we have the wedding?" I ask, plopping down next to him.

"We're already married," he grunts, and I giggle. "But any time you want is fine with me. I'm pretty wide open for the next eight months or so."

"Eight months?" I ask, my brows dipping.

"Training camp," he clarifies.

"You think you'll be going to training camp?"

He shrugs. "It's been my routine for the last decade so I have to make plans with that in mind. When were you thinking?"

"I wanted to do this before the end of the year, but there's no good time with the holidays approaching and Michelle's due date looming right in the middle between Thanksgiving and Christmas."

"Why do you want to do it before the end of the year?"

I lift a shoulder. "Because I'm excited." The end of my sentence sounds more like a question than an answer.

"You sure about that?" he prods.

I blow out a breath. "Because I want to feel beautiful in my dress and if I'm all huge and pregnant I won't."

He reaches over to toss an arm around me, and I snuggle into his chest. "You are growing our child," he reminds me. "I can't think of anything more beautiful than that."

I look up at him, and his eyes are heated as he looks down at me. "How'd I get so lucky to land you?"

He chuckles. "I'm a real, live Prince Charming."

"I'm so glad you finally see it, too."

He smirks at me. "Why don't we wait until after the baby gets here? We'll have our very own little ring bearer."

"*After* the baby?" I repeat. I hadn't really considered that as a possibility.

"What if we do it on our one-year anniversary? It'll be a fresh start, no contracts, just us."

I sit up and turn toward him. "Our one-year anniversary," I whisper.

His brows dip. "Bad idea?"

I shake my head, and I lean forward and press a kiss to his lips. "It's perfect," I murmur against his mouth. I don't even know how I didn't think of it, but the symbolism of reciting our vows to one another all over again on the day when our legally contracted time together would end seems like the perfect way to celebrate our very real love for one another. And to do it in front of family, friends, and our little one...well, I can't think of anything more beautiful than that.

With our date in mind, I get planning. The baby will be almost two months old, plenty of time for me to work off the baby weight—at least I hope so. I find the most adorable onesie that looks like a tux and I can't wait to see him in it.

Time marches forward, and we give thanks around a table with Josh, Nicki, my parents, and Luke's mom, who rented a house about fifteen minutes from our place for now. She wants to make sure she likes living here before she buys.

A week after Thanksgiving, Jack texts Luke to let him know Michelle went into labor early. Jack Alexander Dalton Junior, or JJ, is born with both his parents there. Michelle's parents, Carol, Luke, and me all hang out in the waiting room for the news, and Jack's eyes shine as he tells us it's a boy.

Gone is the persona of the victorious champion making waves on the field, instead replaced with this brand-new dad. We head in to meet the baby, and Michelle runs a hand along the baby's head. That's when the shiny rock on her hand gleams in the light.

My eyes widen, but I don't say a word.

"This is Jack Junior," she says softly so as not to wake the baby.

I squeeze Luke's hand. For a long time, he thought he would be the daddy in this room. I can't imagine what he's feeling right now, but I'm proud of him for showing up for his brother despite their sordid history on top of the lies and manipulations from Michelle. We can only hope she changes her selfish ways for the sake of this baby, and seeing her hold him the way she is tells me there's already been a monumental shift in her.

I guess motherhood will do that, and I'm excited to find out how it'll affect me in the coming months.

Carol washes her hands at the sink by the door then moves toward Michelle. "May I touch him?" she asks, and she gently tousles the baby's soft fuzz on the top of his head. "He's precious," she says, and she pauses a beat before she lets out a soft gasp with a surprised, "Oh! Your ring..."

Carol's eyes edge over to Jack, who shrugs. "It's Grandma Rose's ring," he admits.

"Are you two..." Carol trails off.

"Engaged?" Michelle finishes. She glances up at Jack. "Yes."

Jack nods and glances down at Michelle.

What?

I try to piece together what's going on, but I can't figure out his intentions here. Just a few weeks ago, he was telling his brother how he has no idea how Luke put up with Michelle for as long as he did...and now they're engaged?

Is this because of the baby?

Because of the inheritance?

Or does Jack actually love Michelle so much that he wants to spend the rest of his life with her?

Do fake marriages run in the family? Is that genetic?

These are all questions I *want* to ask, but social norms prevent me from actually voicing them.

I guess time will tell.

* * *

When I wake up on Christmas morning three weeks later, I can't help but reflect on everything that's happened since last Christmas. I was so excited when I selected Todd in my office Secret Santa. I'd been hardcore crushing on the guy since we started working together, and I was thrilled when he admitted he had feelings for me, too.

We rang in the new year together and I was so hopeful that I'd finally met my prince.

Little did I know just how much my life was going to change. Little did I know that my *actual* prince was right around the corner and I just needed to be patient.

The best thing that ever happened to me was getting dumped and fired in the same day. It sent me flying toward rock bottom, and I never would've moved to Vegas if it hadn't happened. I wouldn't have taken the one-night stand bet with the girls at Nicki's bachelorette party. I still would've met Luke since we were walking down the aisle together, but I doubt we would've ended up together since Todd would've come with me to Vegas as my date to the wedding.

Yet here I am, tangled in Luke's bajillion thread count sheets with his arms wrapped around me. I stare at the lights on the tree we put up here in the bedroom. It was his idea, not mine—but there's nothing more romantic than making love under the glowing lights of that tree.

Last night I wondered how good old Todd was doing along with my former best work friend, Brittany. I haven't spoken to either of them since the day I was fired. On the one hand, I don't blame her for wanting to keep her distance from me since she still has to work with Belinda every day. On the other hand, my life changed at a whirlwind pace. It's not like I was scrambling to the phone to call her, either.

So I looked up Todd on Facebook. We're not friends anymore, obviously—especially not after he went to the media early in my relationship with Luke to disprove our engagement's legitimacy—but I spotted a picture of him *with* Brittany. They looked awfully cozy for former colleagues.

But the thing about it is...I didn't feel an ounce of jealousy. A year ago, I would've lost my shit if my best friend started dating the guy I had a crush on forever, but I've ended up in the right place. And so all I can do is hope for the best for them, too.

"Good morning," Luke says, his deep voice raspy from sleep. "Merry Christmas." He leans over and presses a soft kiss to my neck, and chills run down my legs.

"Merry Christmas," I whisper back, and I turn in his direction. He tightens his grasp around me, and after a Christmas morning romp that's truly a gift, we lie panting beside one another.

"How different will Christmas morning next year look?" Luke asks.

"Very," I say as I try to picture it. "We'll have an eight-month-old."

"And you'll probably be knocked up with number two."

I smack his arm. "Let's just take it one baby at a time. What was your Christmas last year like? And did you ever think this one would look like it does?"

He laughs. "It was...interesting. And no. I never could've dreamed up this one."

"What does *interesting* mean?"

"It's an adjective. It means catching someone's attention," he deadpans.

I purse my lips at him and wait for him to get to the truth.

"Michelle was here. We were still together. I had Christmas Day off, but I had practice the day before and the day after, and then we had a home game the day after that. We went to her mom's house for a Christmas luncheon and it was over the top extravagant. Calvin bought Michelle a car, which put my diamond earrings to shame. It was just...nothing I am. I spent the day pretending to be happy when I was miserable. Everyone in the Bennett family grilled me as to why Michelle and I weren't engaged."

"How'd you field those questions?" I ask, tracing a circle on his chest.

"I told people I wasn't getting married again, that I'd been through it once and wouldn't do it again."

"Enter Ellie."

He laughs. "I couldn't resist that cute little ass of yours."

"You married me for my ass?"

"And your tits." He reaches for one of them. I purse my lips, and he lets out a soft chuckle. "I wouldn't have had the idea to do it even for pretend if I didn't like *everything* about you the second I met you."

Heat prickles behind my eyes at his words. "That might be the sweetest thing you've ever said to me."

"A true Prince Charming," he jokes. "Speaking of which, let's go see if Santa came."

I narrow my eyes at him. "You think he did?"

He shrugs as his eyes twinkle, and I feel like I've reverted back twenty years or so as excitement races through me on this Christmas morning.

We head down to the family room, where a ridiculously large tree sits in one corner. We have five trees up in different places throughout the house, and since Luke has a bum knee and I'm pregnant, we hired help to get them all up along with lights decorating the outside of our house.

I think about his words from this morning and how different next year will look. Will we have Paw Patrol characters on our front lawn? Mickey Mouse? Snoopy?

Maybe all three.

Pepper lays near the tree, but when she spots us, her tail wags out of control as she gets up and races over to Luke. He chuckles, and I stare at the bottom of the tree.

This Christmas morning is different from my others as we start our own traditions together. I always went to my parents' house and spent the day with them—which we're doing, but they wanted us to have our own family Christmas mornings first, so we're going over in the early evening to celebrate. Carol will be joining us, and Michelle has even said she might stop by so baby JJ can see some of his extended family on Christmas along with his Grammy Carol.

Jack is playing today, so he won't be stopping by—another one of those life events that the guys on the field have to miss out on. While I want Luke to play if that's what he wants, I'd hate for him to miss his son's first Christmas. I think back to Nadine's words of advice to Nicki at the bachelorette party that football careers are short and retirement is long, and I can't help but wonder what Luke's thinking as his knee gets stronger and stronger every day.

He hands me a box, and I unwrap it to find a canvas print from our wedding day. It's a beautiful shot of us on the beach as the sun sets behind us, and despite everything that happened that day, it's still a beautiful memory. It was the day he admitted he had real feelings for me even though we didn't enter our marriage the traditional way.

He opens the matching daddy t-shirt and baby onesie I bought—the leprechaun from Lucky Charms for Luke, naturally, and a pot of gold for the baby.

We both open too many gifts from each other, from jewelry to books to electronics, and he hands me a small box last as we sit in the middle of a mound of wrapping paper that Pepper skips around happily in. I lift the lid off the box and find an envelope, and I pull out a stack of papers from it.

First is Luke's amended will with me as his primary beneficiary.

Second is a business plan for Dalton Athlete Management along with an LLC by the same name.

Third is a piece of paper that simply says, "this is only the start" in Luke's neat handwriting.

My brows draw together in confusion as I look up at him. "The start?" I ask.

He stretches out his knee. He bends it then straightens it again. It's doing so much better even though he still has more therapy to get it back to playing shape. "I've had a lot of time to think over the last couple months," he begins. "And I know what I want my future to look like."

My brows rise in surprise.

"I never thought beyond the game, and not because it was bad luck but because there was nothing else I loved more. There was nothing I cared about more than playing. And then I met you. It's as simple and as complicated as that. I want to be with you and with him." He nods toward my stomach. "I haven't even met him yet and I already love him more than whatever happens on the field. And if I could love someone that much before I even meet him, then I know I need to be around for all of it."

"All of it?" I echo.

He nods. "I'm going to work my ass off to get healthy for you and for him, not to play. Even if Coach and the GM and Calvin get together and invite me to play again...the answer will be no. Because this is only the start of our life together, and I won't let football or injuries or families or crazy exes or *anything* come between us. I'm retiring."

"Wow," I say softly, not sure what else to say as my heart thumps in my chest. "You're...you're giving up your career for me?"

He shakes his head. "For us. It's not guaranteed anyway, and I'd rather go out on my terms than dick around for the next eight months with unknown answers. We don't have time for that, not when we could be building our business as we wait for our baby's arrival."

We don't have time for that.

He's talking excitedly and with animation in terms of *we* and the future, and it's honestly the most beautiful gift anyone has ever given me. My heart squeezes with love for him.

"Are you sure about this?" I ask, not because I want him to rethink it or because I want him to play but because I don't want him to make a rash decision when playing is all he's ever wanted out of life. I think back to his reaction when Savannah sent the story about his drug test to the press and how his first concern is that it would kill his reputation and nobody would want them on his team. He wanted to play as little as a couple months ago, but something changed.

The baby.

He nods slowly. "There's too much risk. If I take another hit to my knee, it would be devastating. I take unnecessary risks every time I step out onto that field, but it didn't matter when it was just me. I can't continue to take those risks when I have two people who need me."

His words are so simple, yet they tell me everything.

He isn't just giving up the game. He's giving up everything he loves because he found something he loves even more.

Our game plan may have started with a fake engagement, but happily ever after is our end game.

EPILOGUE

We're lying around lazily on my parents' couch in their new Vegas place later that evening. Too many presents have been unwrapped, the mass of wrapping paper has been cleaned up, and the food has been eaten.

We're all in turkey comas since my mom always makes a Christmas turkey, and we're sipping hot chocolate with marshmallows as we stare into the crackling flames of the fireplace. The tree glows with lights beside it, and piles of open presents litter the floor (both babies made out pretty well). I'm leaning into my husband's chest as we simply relax.

Josh and Nicki are beside us while my parents clean the kitchen. I asked a hundred times if I could help, and I even tried to start the dishes, but my dad bumped me out of the way and told me to take a load off my feet. I gladly accepted, and I haven't felt this content in a long time.

It's nice having my mom and dad close, and I know that'll only continue to ring true once the baby arrives.

My mom sits on one of the easy chairs across from the couch, and my dad takes the one beside her. They both hold their own mugs of hot chocolate between their hands.

"Time for the annual Nolan Trip down Memory Lane," my dad says.

"Best memory of the year?" my mom asks. She glances around as she waits for one of us to answer.

"Marrying Nicki," Josh says.

"Aww," Nicki says, and she leans in for a kiss. "Mine was finding out about this little nugget," she says, rubbing her stomach. She's due in under two months now.

"Thanks a lot," Josh says.

"Marrying you goes without saying," she says, elbowing him playfully as he narrows his eyes at her. "Okay, let me amend that since apparently it doesn't go without saying. Marrying you, the honeymoon, and finding out about the baby. In no particular order."

"Moving to Las Vegas. It's a new adventure for us," my dad says, looking at my mom, "and it's wonderful to land so close to both our kids."

My mom nods. "I can't choose one, but the weddings, the grandbabies, and moving here." She glances at me. "Which reminds me...we never got to have that big celebration for *your* wedding."

I sit up a little. "Hey, you're right. Why don't we have one next year?" I ask, turning to Luke.

He grins. "How's June twenty-first sound?"

I pretend to think for all of a half a second. "That sounds like *perfection*."

We both laugh, and my parents look at us like they don't get the inside joke.

"We'd like to formally invite you to our wedding, round two, on June twenty-first," I say. "I want your help planning and picking out a dress," I say to my mom. "I'd be honored if you'd walk me down the aisle," I say to my dad. I turn to Nicki. "I want you to be my maid of honor."

"And I want you to be my best man," Luke says to Josh. "Again."

"Our baby boy will be there, and so will his cousins, and it'll be the most perfect way to celebrate our first anniversary with a real wedding in front of all our family and friends," I finish.

My mom claps her hands together with excitement and my dad looks proudly at the two of us. We share a round of hugs before my dad turns to me. "So tell us your best part of the year."

I smile softly. "It's a tie between the night Luke ripped up the contract for our fake relationship and the day he found out about the baby."

Luke's eyes twinkle as they land on mine. "Same. And when we found out he's a boy."

"Speaking of these boys," my mom says, "do either of you have names picked out yet?"

I laugh. "We haven't talked about names yet."

Luke shrugs and shakes his head.

"We have one," Nicki says, raising a hand. "Are we telling?"

Josh shrugs. "Go for it."

"Good, then your sister can't try to steal it."

I hold my hands up innocently. "I'm not going to steal it!" There's a name that I keep coming back to in my mind, and I guarantee Josh won't pick it. "Tell us!"

Nicki and Josh exchange another glance, and then Josh says, "Warner."

"Warner?" my dad asks. "Like the great Kurt Warner?"

Josh chuckles. "Yeah."

"Warner," my mom says, turning it over. "Warner Nolan. Oh, that's cute!"

"Middle name?" I ask.

"James, after Dad."

My mom's hand goes to her chest like it's the most adorable thing she's ever heard.

"Dang it!" I mutter. "I wanted James for a middle name."

"Ha ha, we're first so you can't steal it!" Josh singsongs.

"Enjoy going into labor first," I say, and I smirk at Nicki.

"Hey, don't involve me in your weird sibling stuff," Nicki says, and we all laugh.

I guess it's time to start thinking about names.

* * *

We're snuggled together on the couch watching the early Times Square coverage on New Year's Eve with Pepper lying on the floor nearby when he asks, "What was your last New Year's Eve like?"

I lean into him a little more, and he tightens his arm around me. "I was with Todd. We'd just gotten together about a week earlier and we were trying to keep it on the down low because of the office's fraternization policy. But we went to a bar with a big group of friends and he snuck in a kiss at midnight. I drank way too much and was stumbling around wasted. Slightly different from this year."

His arm is wrapped all the way around me and his hand rests on my stomach, and I rest my hand on top of his for a beat.

"How about you?" I ask.

"I was with Michelle. She dragged me to a charity ball. I had to wear a tux." He makes a gagging sound, and I giggle.

"Sounds like torture." I draw a little circle pattern on the back of his hand.

He lifts a shoulder. "It was. I'd been wanting to end things with her but it was just one thing after another. You don't break up a relationship nearly two years strong over Thanksgiving dinner, you know? Or right before Christmas."

"This low key celebration tonight might be the best New Year's Eve I've ever had."

"Same. But I know how to make it even better," he says.

I turn and look up at him, and he looks down at me with that familiar heat in his eyes. "How?" I ask.

He chuckles. "Like you don't know how."

"In front of the dog?" I whisper.

"Pepper!" Luke yells, and the dog startles as she lifts her head. "Go to bed."

I sit up and giggle, and it turns to even bigger laughs when Pepper actually does saunter out of the room. "I think we're alone now."

He reaches for me and pulls my head down to his. He kisses me with passion, with love and adoration, and it's the kind of kiss that makes me see how the lust and the butterflies are still there even after everything we've been through, but there's more. There's a solid base and a real foundation that came from starting with friendship and working through some of life's biggest challenges together.

I pull his shirt over his head and then my own, and it's mere moments before we're both naked and I'm moving over the top of him as gasps and sighs of pleasure fill the room. He thrusts into me, and as our bodies rock together one last time in this year, I give into the pleasure as a climax plows into me with brute force. He follows right behind me, and it's as we're both panting and coming down from the throes of pleasure that I think about the future we're building together. The intimate moments on our couch may be fewer and farther between as our baby starts to grow, or even as the house is filled with more babies. But that just means we'll find new ways to be adventurous and new places to express our passion for one another.

We kiss at midnight, but neither of us tastes even a drop of alcohol as we ring in the new year. I always think of this day as the perfect time to reflect, and while this year has certainly brought me an incredible array of ups and downs, I wouldn't change a moment of it. All those little events added up to this one big emotion I have in my heart for the man beside me, and I'm thankful for every blessing and every challenge that we've gotten to face together.

Whatever tomorrow brings, we'll still have that.

And, by the way, tomorrow brings *good* news for a change.

"Guess what?" Luke says as he saunters into the kitchen. I'm just making scrambled eggs, and he moves toward the coffee pot.

"That's decaf," I warn him. I'm sticking to decaf since I can't give up my coffee addiction altogether but I also can't have too much caffeine.

"Thanks," he says. He pours a cup anyway. "I'll repeat. Guess what?"

I laugh. "What?"

"Savannah married Tristan last night."

My brows dip. "What?"

He nods.

"And how do you feel about that?"

"I feel like celebrating," he says. He does a little dance in the kitchen, and I can't help my laugh. "No more alimony checks! What a way to start the year."

"Well congratulations. Seems like everything's falling into place."

"Except for poor Tristan Higgins," he says. "I tried to warn him, but apparently he didn't listen. He's got a nightmare on his hands now."

"Maybe she's blackmailing him, too," I suggest, and he looks at me like he hadn't thought of that.

"Interesting theory," he says, and his brows dip as he considers it. "He seemed like he was hearing me when I sat him down and told him about my history with Savannah, yet he still married her. Whatever the case, she's someone else's problem now."

"What does that mean?" I slide some bread into the toaster.

He shrugs. "I hope for his sake they have an airtight prenup that protects the nine million signing bonus he got when he was drafted along with his salary." He takes a sip from his steaming coffee mug.

"Best wishes to them," I say. "I hope it's true love."

"So do I, but I doubt it." He walks over to the table and if he wasn't wearing his brace, I'd hardly even know he's recovering from major surgery on his knee. "There's something strange about the two of them getting married so fast."

"The same could be said for us," I point out.

"I guess you're right." He shrugs as he slides onto his chair. "Oh well. Not my circus, not my monkeys."

"Speaking of monkeys, what do you think of that as a theme for the baby's room?"

"Monkeys?"

I nod as I divvy the eggs out onto two plates.

"Will monkeys make you happy?"

I nod again and smile.

"Then they'll make me happy, too. Happy wife, happy life."

"Man, I really leveled up when I married you." I walk a plate over to him and set it down with a fork.

He nods toward his plate. "Thanks. And don't you forget it."

* * *

We're watching the Aces fight for the AFC championship on a Sunday afternoon a couple weeks later when the back of my brother's jersey catches my eye. The game is tied at three in the middle of the first quarter, and Luke has been vocal about this particular game. He wants to see his team succeed even if he doesn't get to be on the field, and since it's an away game and he's still out, he didn't travel with the team.

"Hey, have you thought of any baby names?" I ask during a commercial break. I haven't really thought too much about it since Christmas at my parents' house, but I'm due three months from today and we still haven't discussed what we're going to name this little jellybean. While Jellybean is cute, I think we should come up with something slightly more traditional.

He shrugs. "There's a few I like. You?"

"I keep coming back to one, but I feel like you're going to hate it. What names do you like?"

"Emmett, Troy, William..."

"Football names?" I ask, wrinkling my nose.

He shrugs innocently. "I have a bunch more if you hate those. What's yours?"

I clear my throat as I get a little nervous to tell him. It's how I've been referring to him in my head whenever I'm not referring to him as Jellybean. "Nolan," I finally say.

He pauses a beat, and he tilts his head like he's rolling it over. "Like your maiden name?"

I nod.

"Nolan Dalton," he says, trying it on for size, and my heart races as I wait for his reaction. "Middle name?"

I shrug. "I was thinking James after my dad, but if I get first, you can take middle. Just please not Troy. I may not know much about football, but I was raised in a Bears' house, not a Cowboys'."

He still hasn't reacted to my name other than to repeat it, and his eyes edge to the screen as the game comes back on.

He laughs. "I actually have a middle name in mind, and it isn't Troy."

"What is it?"

"Oh shit!" he yells as his eyes widen at the screen, and even though we're having what I deem a very important conversation, I glance over to see what he's oh-shitting about.

Someone in a black uniform with red lettering is down, but I can't tell who it is. A ring of players surrounds him as the trainers rush out.

"Who is it?" I practically screech as I pray it isn't my brother.

"Tristan."

I send up a little prayer in my head that he'll be okay. I know now what it's like to help a football player heal, and it's been hard enough helping someone who was nearing the end of his career anyway. I can't imagine the level of disappointment for a kid in his rookie season to get hurt. I pray that whatever it is won't keep him down, that he'll sit out a play or two and then get right back into the game.

That doesn't happen.

The broadcasters show the replay, and my stomach turns over as I see the angle at which his ankle bends. It's not natural. It's not supposed to move like that.

"Fuck," Luke mutters as he shakes his head.

"How long will that keep him out?" I ask.

"Depends on whether it's a compound fracture." We watch as the cart comes out to help haul Tristan off the field. He's covering his face with a towel, and after they move him onto the cart, he lowers the towel to wave to the crowd and let them know he'll be okay. His eyes are rimmed in red and the emotion is written all over his face. This is a devastating blow to Tristan and also to the entire Aces' organization.

"What's a compound fracture?"

"When the bone breaks the skin," he says, and I get a little queasy at that description.

We listen to the broadcasters. "The Aces already lost Luke Dalton to a season-ending injury, and it's looking like Higgins will be out a while, too. You think he'll be back in time for next season?" one of them asks the other.

"Hard to tell, Al, but I'd guess he'll be down a few months. I was talking to Mitch Thompson last night and he said Luke Dalton is making great progress. They're hopeful he'll be ready at the start of next season, but I gotta tell you, I've been hearing rumors about retirement."

"I wouldn't blame the guy," the other broadcaster says. "He's in his thirties now, he's been injured twice. That's a lot to come back from."

I glance at Luke and wait for the broadcasters to cut to commercial before I ask my question. "Are you going to talk to Coach sometime?"

He shrugs. "I'm on contract through the end of this season. My decision doesn't matter right now, and I'm not going to burden him when they're in the middle of playoffs."

"But you *are* going to tell him, right?"

He chuckles and he reaches for my hand. He squeezes it. "If you're worried I'm going to change my mind, I won't. I'm done playing. Not forever...I mean, I'll toss the ball around with Nolan, and maybe I'll coach his peewee league team or middle school or even high school."

My eyes fill with tears as I gaze at him. "You called him *Nolan.*"

His eyes twinkle back at me. "That's his name, isn't it?"

I can't help when I attack him with a very aggressive hug.

The future is looking beautifully bright for Luke, Ellie, and Nolan Dalton.

ACKNOWLEDGMENTS

Thank you to my husband for everything you do. The support, encouragement, and love is what makes this possible. Thank you to my kids for nap time and quiet time when mommy gets to write, and thank you to my parents who love hanging out with my babies so I can get some computer time in.

Thank you to Trenda London from It's Your Story Content Editing, Diane Holtry and Alissa Riker for beta reading, Najla Qamber for the gorgeous cover design, and Katie Harder-Schauer from Proofreading by Katie.

Thank you to Wildfire Marketing, my ARC team, Team LS, and all the bloggers who read, post, and review.

Thank you to you, the reader, for taking time out of your life to spend it with Ellie and Luke. I hope you enjoyed what you read, and I can't wait for you to read what I'm working on next. And who knows? Maybe Jack has a story to tell someday...

ABOUT THE AUTHOR

Lisa Suzanne is a romance author who resides in Arizona with her husband and two kids. She's a former high school English teacher and college composition instructor. When she's not cuddling or chasing her kids, she can be found working on her latest book or watching reruns of *Friends*.

ALSO BY LISA SUZANNE

A LITTLE LIKE DESTINY
A Little Like Destiny Book One
#1 Bestselling Rock Star Romance

TAKE MY HEART
My Favorite Band Book One
#1 Bestselling Rock Star Romance